BOOK 7

CRAIG HALLORAN

DON'T FORGET YOUR FREE BOOKS

Join my newsletter and receive three magnificent stories from my bestselling series for FREE!

Not to mention that you'll have direct access to my collection of over 80 books, including audiobooks and boxsets. FREE and .99 cents giveaways galore!

Sign up here!

WWW.DRAGONWARSBOOKS.COM

Finally, please leave a review of BATTLEGROUND-Book 7 when you finish. I've typed my fingers to the bone writing it and your reviews are a huge help!

BATTLEGROUND REVIEW LINK! THANKS!

Dragon Wars: Monarch Madness - Book 7

By Craig Halloran

★★★★

Amazon Edition

TWO-TEN BOOK PRESS

PO Box 4215, Charleston, WV 25364

ISBN eBook: 978-1-946218-78-0

ISBN Paperback: 979-8-649899-65-9

ISBN Hardback: 978-1-946218-79-7

wwwdragonwarsbooks.com

Publisher's Note

This book is a work of fiction. Names, characters, places, and incidents either are the product of the author's imagination or are used fictitiously, and any resemblance to actual persons, living or dead, events, or locales is entirely coincidental.

❀ Created with Vellum

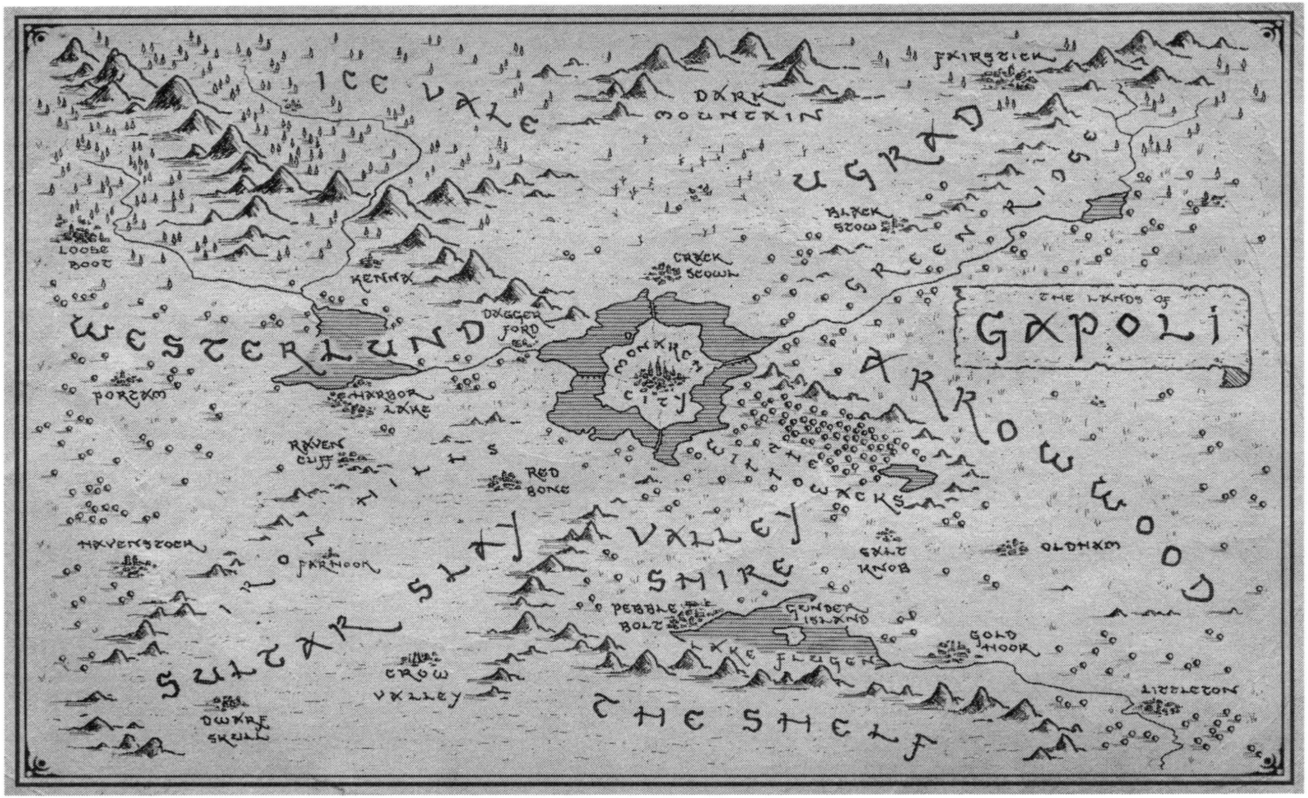
The Lands of
Gapoli
Ice Vale
Dark Mountain
Fairstick
Ugrad
Green Ridge
Black Stow
Crack Scowl
Loose Boot
Kenna
Dagger Ford
Westerlund
Monarch City
Portam
Harbor Lake
Raven Cliff
Iron Hills
Red Bone
The Willowacks
Arrow Wood
Havenstock
Farmoor
Sultar Slay
Valley Shire
Salt Knob
Oldham
Pebble Bolt
Gunder Island
Lake Flugen
Gold Hook
Crow Valley
Dwarf Skull
The Shelf
Littleton

MONARCH CITY

Dragons glided slowly in a circle in the skies above Monarch Castle. Their tremendous wings beat occasionally, keeping them afloat in the stiff wind on an otherwise gray and rainy day. Dozens of dragons had their talons latched onto the castle's walls and battlements. Most of them were middling dragons with black wings, scales like armor, and claws and teeth that shredded metal. Only a few grand dragons were on the grounds.

Grey Cloak brushed his hair out of his eyes. He stood inside the kitchen tower that the elven servant Sayma had taken him to earlier. The small tower gave him a full view of the action in the courtyard. He wasn't alone either. Zora stood by his side, staring out the portal window, shoulder to shoulder with him, her eyes wide.

"I've never seen so many dragons," she said, her voice trembling. "My stomach twists in my belly."

"Don't worry. I'll protect you," he replied as he patted Streak, who was latched to his back underneath his cloak, on the head. The dragon's throat rattled. "I mean *we'll* protect you."

"Huh," she said with a nervous laugh. "If your attempt at humor is to soothe me, it didn't work. Well, maybe a tad."

Grey Cloak smirked. His eyes were fixed on the situation quickly unraveling in the courtyard. Rows of Riskers and their dragons were on the ground. They were face to face with ranks of Monarch Knights and Honor Guard. The soldiers stood in a rigid formation, and they'd laid their weapons down at their sides. They grumbled as the greatly built Riskers, fully armored, wearing their dragon helms fashioned from dark metal, strutted before them. One of the Riskers, a brown-bearded man, had unrolled a scroll and was announcing the terms of Monarch Castle's surrender.

"They should still be fighting," Grey Cloak said as many of the fingertips of Monarch Castle's finest twitched at their sides. "They want to fight."

"Look at all of those dragons," Zora said. "They wouldn't stand a chance against them, would they?"

"They gave up too easily. Bloody Monarchs are making them stand down, just like Tatiana said." His stomach twisted. "How can they betray their own people?"

"I don't know, but it's happening." She peered up at the higher levels of the castles, where men and women in lavish clothing wore stone-cold expressions. "The Monarchs are a strange breed."

"It appears that the Monarchs are only looking out for themselves. That's not strange at all. They are only embracing their selfish nature."

She looked at him with disappointment in her big green eyes and said, "I meant strange looking. It's obvious they are selfish. Look at their gaudy clothing."

He managed a chuckle and said, "It's only a matter of time until Black Frost strips them of that." Grabbing her hand, he started toward the narrow spiral steps. "Come on, let's get back to the others."

"Is that when you are going to reveal your master plan that will save all of us and Monarch City?" she quipped.

"Something like that," he said casually.

"Why don't you tell me now?"

"Uh, I'm still filling in the details. I'll have it ready by the time I'm there."

Zora rolled her eyes. "Sure, if you say so."

Streak nipped his ear as they reached the bottom.

"Ow! What did you do that for?" he asked, rubbing his ear.

Streak stretched his scaly neck toward a kitchen table full of baskets of bread. His pink tongue flicked out of his mouth.

Grey Cloak grabbed a roll and fed it to the broad runt dragon. "Here. And don't bite me again."

Streak gobbled the roll down whole and beckoned with his tongue for more.

He grabbed the basket and fed the dragon along the way. "Save some for Dyphestive. And I mean it—don't bite me again."

On cats' feet, he and Zora stole their way back toward Codd's Crypt, where the others were waiting, without being seen. The halls were empty of servants and soldiers, as they had all gathered near the courtyard to watch their fate unfold.

The two sword masters, Jakoby and Reginald the Razor, stood guard at the crypt door. Jakoby's hard eyes fastened on Grey Cloak's, and he asked, "Is it true? Do the Monarchs surrender?"

Grey Cloak nodded. "The Monarch Knights and Honor Guard are being made to surrender while the Monarchs watch from their high terraces. It's bad, Jakoby. I'm sorry."

Jakoby hung his head. "I might have fallen out with my brethren, but I never would have foreseen this. The Monarch Knights would never surrender. They would die first. Someone is behind this."

Razor grabbed a roll out of the basket, and Streak rattled his neck at him. "I've been doing my fair share of fighting, too, little dragon. I'm hungry too."

Streak flicked his tongue at him.

Razor flicked his back and ate the roll. "If I'm going to die, I'm going to die with a full belly." He glanced at Zora. "And perhaps with one final kiss too."

Zora patted his cheek, smiled, and said, "A full belly will have to do." She opened the door and went into the crypt.

Grey Cloak followed her, leaving Jakoby and Razor stationed outside. They were greeted by Dyphestive, Tatiana, and Leena when they entered. Leena the monk was standing near Irsk Mondo and Fenton Slay, who were sitting propped up against the outer columns, bound with glowing cords of magic. Fenton was out cold, but Irsk was wide awake.

Irsk winked at Zora and asked, "Did you miss me?"

"Why didn't you *muzzle* him?" Zora yelled at Tatiana.

The beautiful elven servant of the Wizard Watch cast her eyes down on her friend and said, "He chewed through the rope and swallowed it. He's part goblin, remember."

"He's a fiend." Zora turned her back on Irsk. "I don't want to hear another word out of him."

"Ow!" Irsk moaned.

Leena, a monk with long, cherry-red hair, had started whacking Irsk in the head with her nunchaku. The twin sticks spun quickly as she beat the long-limbed part goblin, part elf like a drum.

"I'll be quiet! I'll be quiet!" Irsk cowered. The beating stopped. The slimy-tongued Irsk said politely, "Apologies, Zora. I'm sorry for all that I've put you through."

"I don't care," she said.

"It seems you do," Irsk replied.

Tatiana spun Zora away from Irsk's creepy gaze and said, "Let Leena handle him. She's good at it." She turned her attention to Grey Cloak as well. "What is going on out there?"

"The soldiers have laid down their weapons. The Monarchy is in full surrender," Grey Cloak replied.

"We can't let that happen," Dyphestive said, gripping his war mace. "Won't they fight?"

"If they fight, they will die," Tatiana warned. "We need to find a way out of here now. I came for you two." She pointed at Grey Cloak and Dyphestive. "We must leave and fight another day."

"I take it Than never returned?" Grey Cloak asked as he scanned the room.

"No," Tatiana said. "We have more important matters to worry about now."

Dyphestive turned his back on Tatiana and stared up at the statue of Codd. "I'm not leaving. He wouldn't leave either. He'd fight."

"You don't know that," Tatiana said urgently. "Listen to me. The Monarchs have chosen their side. We can't change that. Not now."

"They chose the wrong side!" Dyphestive said. He climbed up on Codd's pedestal and started removing the thigh guard of Codd's armor. It was as big as a shield.

Tatiana shook her head. "Grey Cloak, reason with him. We are running out of time." She stared deep into his eyes. "Do you want to win the battle or win the war?"

"I think you should do what she says. I would," Irsk said coolly.

Zora gave Irsk a nasty look. "Leena, can you sew his lips up?"

Leena raised her pointed eyebrows.

"Consider my lips sealed," Irsk said as he scooted away from Leena's fearless gaze. "She scares me."

Tatiana continued her argument. "The longer we wait, the harder it will be to get out of here. We must find a way to get out now," she urged.

Grey Cloak paced with his hands behind his back and thumbs rolling. "If we don't try to stop them now, we might not ever get them out. There has to be a way. There is always a way."

"You know dragons as well as any. Grands that can take out an entire city out there. Do you really think that you can stop them? And the Riskers, some of which are just like you? It's not possible. We must flee."

"I'm tired of running," Dyphestive said. He'd managed to remove one of Codd's bracers and strap it over his arm. "No more running."

"This is not the time and place to fight." Tatiana's cheeks flushed. "And the time will never come if we don't leave now. We need to focus on the Dragon Charms. Trust the Wizard Watch, Grey Cloak and Dyphestive. It's the only way."

Grey Cloak shook his head. "We need to buy time. If we buy time, the Sky Riders will come. I know it."

"Is that your plan? Waiting for the Sky Riders to show?" Zora asked with a huff. "I could have thought up that one."

"They'll show. I know they will. Didn't the Wizard Watch warn them too?"

"You can't count on them!" Tatiana yelled. "You need to trust me now. It's time to quit arguing."

"Of course we can count on them. They are here to protect us," Grey Cloak said adamantly. "They would never let this happen if they could prevent it."

Tatiana clenched her fists, and with fire in her eyes, she asked, "Why won't you listen to me? Why are you so stubborn?"

Grey Cloak eyed her and approached. "What aren't you telling me, Tatiana? What is it? Did the Wizard Watch have a falling out with the Sky Riders?"

"The Sky Riders are dead!" Tatiana shouted. "Black Frost killed them! He killed all of them!"

Zora gasped, Grey Cloak's jaw dropped, and Irsk Mondo's chuckles echoed throughout the crypt.

3

Tatiana took a deep breath and said, "I'm sorry. I didn't want to tell you like this, but you gave me no choice."

Grey Cloak's face had paled. He'd lost feeling in his extremities and barely managed to get out, "All of them? It can't be all of them. How do you know this?"

"I wouldn't say it if I hadn't seen it with my own eyes," Tatiana said quietly as she watched Zora put an arm around Grey Cloak's waist while Dyphestive put a hand on his shoulder. "We were supposed to meet with Justus. He is the one we communicated regularly with. He didn't show. We investigated."

Grey Cloak looked up and met her eyes. "What did you find?"

"There was a great battle—Sky Riders against the

Riskers, dragon against dragon. Even the Gunder giants fought. Hidemark was destroyed, all of the Sky Riders and their dragons with them. The entire forest was incinerated."

He responded with disbelief in his tone, "That's impossible. No dragon could have done that sort of damage."

"Even Garthar, king of the giants, was destroyed. Giant skin is resistant to dragon fire, but Black Frost's flame was too hot," she said.

"Black Frost did it?" Dyphestive asked. "He was there?"

"Our spies in Dark Mountain have confirmed it. It wasn't hard to learn, as the Riskers are glad to boast about the great devastation that Black Frost wrought. He stands invincible." Tatiana offered a sympathetic look. "I am very sorry. We all are sorry, but Grey Cloak, you are the last Sky Rider left."

He pulled away from his friends and said, "I can't believe they are gone. Justus, Arik, Mayzie, Stayzie, Hammerjaw, Yuri, Fomander, Hogrim... and Anya? Was she there too?"

"We believe so," she said.

"But she was with me. When did this happen?"

"Months ago, perhaps longer. The crater still smolders like a volcano, so it is difficult to tell."

"Months ago!" He poked his chest. "Are you telling me this happened months ago and I'm only finding out about it now?"

"It wouldn't have made any difference," she tried to say with sympathy, but she had a knack for being cold and direct. "This is why we need to leave now."

"Well, as the fire heats up, the batter thickens," Irsk commented.

Leena clocked him on the head with her nunchaku.

"Ow! You bloody barefooted devil. Quit doing that. I'm a talker."

Dyphestive's mouth hung open, and he shook his head. With deep sadness in his voice, he said, "I can't believe Anya is dead. And Cinder too?"

"Black Frost's flame is unlike anything that we've ever seen before. Again, I'm sorry. I know they were your friends, especially Anya. But we need both of you alive—to help fight Black Frost when the time comes." Tatiana pleaded with them the best that her personality would allow. "You have to trust me."

Zora took Grey Cloak and Dyphestive by the hands and said, "I'm sorry to say this, but she is right. We can't fight them, not now. We need to escape and plan."

"The Wizard Watch told the Monarchs what happened at Gunder Island. I believe that is why they surrendered. They are scared."

"Or compliant," Dyphestive added. He moved back to the statue of Codd with an angry look on his face and started stripping armor from the towering statue's body like a man possessed.

"What is he doing?" Tatiana asked.

"I don't know, but he's been obsessed with Codd ever since he bought that little statue," Grey Cloak said. "Dyphestive, now isn't the time for that."

His words fell on deaf ears, and Dyphestive continued to remove more parts of the polished ancient armor.

"Everyone vents in one way or the other," Grey Cloak said. "Let him be."

Out of the corner of his eye, he caught Irsk watching Dyphestive with avid interest. The leader of the Dark Addler caught Grey Cloak looking and turned away.

With his eyes remaining on Irsk, he said, "Sky Riders or no Sky Riders, we can't stand here and do nothing. We have to inspire the soldiers and fight the Riskers before they dig in."

Jakoby popped his head in the door. He had a concerned look on his face and said, "The soldiers are on the move. Sounds like they are coming this way. We even saw some yonders flying by." His gaze landed on Dyphestive. "What in the other side of the flaming fence are you doing, Dyphestive? Take that helmet off! It's sacred!"

Dyphestive's head was big compared to a normal man's, but it was swallowed up by Codd's helm. He held the bottom rim with two hands and wiggled his head inside. "I almost fit," he said. "Codd really was a big, big man."

"He was an ogre," Jakoby said as he moved deeper into the chamber. "That's why no one else could ever wear the armor. No other knight matched up in size. The legends say he was as big as a giant, but the armor shows otherwise."

"I thought it wasn't the size of the body that mattered," Tatiana commented as she combed her long fingers through her ponytail. "Dalsay told me it's the size of the heart that matters."

"That's true, but his heart isn't big enough to fill that breastplate," Jakoby said, watching Dyphestive try to fit into it. "No one's is."

"It's not very heavy," Dyphestive said as he slipped on one of the gauntlets. He flexed the polished metal fingers.

Razor entered the room and closed the door behind him, smiling at the group. "They are coming."

"We've wasted too much time," Tatiana said as she fished the Star of Light from one of her pouches and faced the door. "We have nowhere to run now. Everyone, come to me. I can conceal us."

Dyphestive said as he watched the gauntlet shrink over his hand, "Grey Cloak, everyone, look—the armor is shrinking!"

Everyone turned and faced Dyphestive and slowly looked upward.

Grey Cloak lifted his eyebrows and said, "Brother, the armor isn't shrinking. You're growing."

4

Dyphestive watched as his comrades shrank. His helmet bumped against the crypt's domed stone ceiling. With his head tilted at an angle, he gazed upon his gaping friends and asked, "How do I look?"

"Ginormous!" Zora said.

"Glorious," Grey Cloak added.

The whites of Jakoby's eyes were bright. "There is a prophecy of the ancients that has been told and retold for centuries."

"What does it say?" Dyphestive asked in a deep voice.

"The blood of Codd trickles through many rivers and streams, losing itself, only to find itself in the time of need. Codd's blood breathes life into metal. Codd's blood burns like the fires of a furnace. Codd's blood will purify and diminish. Codd's heartbeats are never-ending." With sweat beading on his forehead, Jakoby took a knee. "You are an heir of Codd. I swear my sword to your service. You are the one the Monarch Knights have been waiting for."

"I am?" Dyphestive asked. His blood ran hot as he opened and closed the metal fingers of Codd's gauntlet. The armor fit his body like a glove, and his heart beat like thunder. He stared down at the statue of Codd. "I'm huge," he said in a cavernous voice.

"That's an understatement," Grey Cloak said. "Dyphestive grows and the armor with him. "How is this possible?

Tatiana held the Star of Light and said, "It is ancient magic that Dyphestive's body has activated, but it won't last forever."

Razor closed the door behind him and sealed them inside the crypt. "Company is on the way, and I don't think our big friend can do much for us from in here. Look at him—he can't even fit back through the door."

Dyphestive began fitting more pieces of armor over his body. He strapped on the thigh and shin guards then added the gauntlet and bracer to his other arm. After eyeing the sword belt around the statue's waist, he unbuckled it and strapped it to his waist. He also grabbed his war mace and tucked it into his belt. It was little more than a stick to him since he'd become so large. He stood at full height, eyeballed the exit, and said, "I don't need a door. I'll make my own." Bracing his hands against the stone dome above him, he started to push. The seams between the dome and the walls started to crack and chip. Hunks of stone rained down.

"Dyphestive, stop this!" Tatiana shouted. "We need a plan."

"When you're this big, you don't need a plan." Dyphestive's mighty arms were the size of tree trunks, but they still trembled as he clenched his teeth and pushed.

With his hands cupped around his mouth, Grey Cloak hollered up at him, "Use your legs."

Dyphestive glanced at his blood brother and nodded. "Ah, as you say, little brother." His legs heaved under him. "Hurk!"

The crypt's dome popped off at the rim. The red-cheeked Dyphestive shoved the huge lid over to the side, then he grabbed Codd's shield and started to climb out of the crypt.

"Dyphestive, you don't know how long the magic will last," Tatiana said.

"And?"

She gave him an awkward look as she leaned back from his gaze and said, "Be careful."

The soldiers hammered at the crypt's doors.

"These doors are going to give!" Razor said.

The doors crashed open, and well-armed Monarch Knights spilled in.

Razor spun his blades before their eyes. "Welcome to the party!"

The knights stopped dead in their tracks as they stared upward.

"Do my eyes deceive me?" the knight commander, who had a red-plumed helmet, asked. "Is that Codd?"

Dyphestive caught the knight commander's words and saluted. "I'm not Codd, but now I know what it feels like to be him." He rose to his full height. "Who's going to help me take back Monarch Castle from these flying devils?"

The Monarch Knights lifted their swords high. With new fire in their eyes, they let out a unified cheer. "Long live the Monarchy!"

Dyphestive said at the top of his lungs, "Long live the Monarchy!"

The crypt was located on the back side of the castle's outer wall. When he turned, he came face to face with the soldiers manning the wall. Their eyes were bigger than saucers.

"Well, little men, are you going to stand there and gawk or help me fight the dragons?"

The soldiers on the wall started shouting. It spread from one soldier to another as more and more of the Honor Guard joined in. In seconds, all the men and women posted on the castle wall were screaming at the top of their lungs.

Dyphestive set his eyes on the dragons circling in the sky. He shook his fist then reached down and drew his sword and said, "It's thunder time!"

5

Commander Shaw, leader of the Riskers, was overseeing the Monarchs' surrender when the loud cheers from the castle walls began. Though slender in build, the brown-haired, middle-aged warrior was as intimidating as anyone in his black plate-mail armor. He fixed his gaze on the Monarch's Knight in front of him. The knight was older, like him, well built, and had a neatly trimmed black beard. He wore a sea-blue cape with white trim and carried a helmet with a white plume in the crook of his arm.

Lifting an eyebrow, Commander Shaw asked, "What is happening?"

"I don't know," the Monarch Knight commander said as sweat ran down his temple. "We've laid our weapons down. I can't imagine what stirs them now."

"Silence them, or I'll silence you."

The Monarch Knight commander swallowed and said, "I'll quiet them at once."

"You'd better do it at once," Dirklen said. He was standing to the right of Commander Shaw, his father, and was clad in the blackened armor of the Riskers. His wavy blond hair was in tangles from flying on a dragon, and his voice was full of venom. "Or I'll personally stick your head on the battlements."

The Monarch Knight commander dared a look but quickly averted his eyes. "Sergeant Tinnison, silence your Honor Guard patrolling the walls!"

The stocky Honor Guard in scale-mail armor stepped away from the ranks of his men, saluted, and said, "At once!"

Dirklen's bright-eyed twin sister, Magnolia, twisted her long blond hair with a finger and eyed the sky. "The dragons see something." She pointed toward the barrier walls. "Something over there has caught their attention."

"That something will die!" Dirklen said.

The ground trembled beneath their feet. *Thooom! Thooom!*

"What is that?" Dirklen asked. He glared at the Monarch Knight commander. "What is that?"

"I don't know, young sire. I swear it!" the Monarch Knight commander answered.

The Monarchs in the terraces above them were bent over the walls and pointing below, watching the activity.

"Father, what is it?" Dirklen demanded.

He gave his son an irritated glance and said, "It's Commander Shaw." He turned his attention to the wall behind the ranks of surrendering Monarch Knights and Honor Guards. "And I have no idea what it is."

The ground trembled faster as the thunderous steps came closer and louder.

Thoom-Thoom-Thoom-Thoom- Thoom!

The Monarchs screamed as a section of castle wall exploded outward. *Boom!*

A giant knight in full armor burst through the wall like a juggernaut. The soldiers on the walls screamed like their lungs were bursting.

The giant knight stopped and pointed his sword at Commander Shaw. "Leave now, or I'll put an end to all of you!"

Magnolia squinted and asked, "Is that Dyphestive?" Her breath caught. "It is!"

The ranks of knights and Honor Guard started to murmur. "It's Codd. Codd is alive! Long live Codd!" some screamed. They reached down for their weapons.

Dirklen spun on his heel and faced his dragon, who sat on the ground behind him. The towering grand dragon was fully grown, its scales covered in black-and-blue tortoiseshell patterns. Its chest heaved as it glared down at the Monarch Knights.

"Chartus, kill those traitors."

Chartus's chest expanded, and an orange-red flame spewing from his mouth sent the Monarch Knights scattering. Not all of them escaped. Their hair and armor caught fire, and they rolled on the ground while their fellow knights tried to pat the flames out.

"Nooo!" Dyphestive screamed as he charged Chartus. He covered the distance between them in two giant running steps and sliced at the dragon's neck.

Chartus snaked his neck out of harm's way and unleashed another blast of fiery breath. Dyphestive blocked the flame with his shield and hacked at the dragon with his sword. They battled head to head like horn-locked stags. Using his shield, Dyphestive plowed into the dragon and drove it backward. A sword strike into Chartus's side drew a painful roar from him. The dragon squirted away and crouched low.

"Fight me, you moon-faced coward!" Dirklen fired arrows at Dyphestive. He stood side by side with Magnolia, who was doing the same. The glowing tips of their arrows whistled through the air and exploded into Codd's armor.

Dyphestive laughed. "The tables have turned, you little fleas!" He kicked the ground, slinging cobblestones and dirt on both of them.

Dirklen and Magnolia dove and rolled away.

Out of the corner of his eye, Dyphestive caught another grand dragon charging. He spun around and smacked it hard in the snout with Codd's shield. The explosive impact flipped the dragon head over tail and sent it crashing through the gardens.

The more Dyphestive fought, it seemed the stronger he became. Codd's armor seemed to guide him like the spirit of the man that had once worn it. He had a heightened sense of awareness that fueled his extraordinary limbs. *I like it!*

Dirklen was down on the ground, screaming at the top of his lungs, firing one harmless arrow after the other. Commander Shaw fled the resurgence of the Monarch's troop, which had been revitalized by the appearance of the giant Dyphestive.

Dyphestive let out another thunderous scream. "For the Monarchy!"

The Monarch Knights and Honor Guard lifted their voices and charged the enemy.

Chartus lowered his horns and rushed Dyphestive again. Dyphestive braced himself behind the shield.

The dragon's skull cracked into the metal, but Dyphestive held his ground, but then another grand dragon slipped right behind his legs, and he tripped over the dragon and fell backward. Both grand dragons pounced on him.

6

"Well, I, for one, am not going to stand around here and let the big fella get all of the glory," Razor remarked as he headed for the exit. "Let's do it for the Monarch."

"You aren't going anywhere, Razor. You stay with me," Tatiana ordered. "For the life of me, I don't think any of you understand the stakes. We need to have a plan. We need to escape before it's too late. Giant or no giant, there are still dozens of dragons. Dyphestive can't take them all."

Grey Cloak patted Tatiana on the shoulder. "And that's why we are going to help." He gave a devilish grin and said, "To arms." He nodded at his dragon. "Come on, Streak. I'm with Razor. We can't let Dyphestive have all the glory."

The dragon jumped into his arms.

Tatiana hooked his arm. "You need to listen to me.

There is too much danger. Black Frost has superior strength in numbers. Now is the time to go."

"I'm not leaving Dyphestive behind ever again." He pulled away from her. "Besides, if the odds are stacked against us, I'll use this." He pulled out the Figurine of Heroes.

Tatiana's body stiffened. "I knew I should have destroyed that when I had the chance."

"But you didn't." He smirked and headed for the door. "Follow that noise."

"Wait, Grey Cloak. What about Irsk and Fenton?" Zora asked.

"You can guard them, or you can come with me. They aren't the biggest problem now," he said.

Zora approached Irsk, gave him a nasty stare, squatted down before him, and said, "Don't ever cross me again, or I swear, I'll kill you."

Irsk waved his fingers at her and said, "I'll try to keep it in mind, fearsome one."

Zora put the Ring of Mist to his nose. The tiny metal petals opened, and pollen spat out. Irsk Mondo dropped like a stone.

Grey Cloak led Talon out of Codd's crypt at a sprint. It was clear by the clamor of battle and the roar of dragons that Dyphestive hadn't wasted any time making his presence known. By the time they hit the outer courtyards, several battles were in full swing.

The dragons attacked the guards on the walls with flames, and their Riskers fired arrows.

Dark Mountain's Black Guard, in their crimson tunics over metal armor, engaged the Honor Guard on the ground.

In the middle of the burgeoning battle scene, among flame and smoke, Dyphestive couldn't be missed. The giant-sized warrior was locked in mortal combat with two dragons trying to tear him to shreds. Grey Cloak had seen his brother in trouble before, but the fight appeared grave. One dragon had its tail locked around his brother's throat, and the other had locked its jaws on his leg. The dragons' claws tore into the armor as they tried to rip away the flesh underneath.

"Dyphestive! I'm coming!" Without thinking, he left the others behind, sprinting to his brother's aid. So small, he wasn't sure what he was going to do. His mind raced. *No potions. No flashings.* He had the Figurine of Heroes but didn't want to use it yet.

Streak squirted out of his arms and dashed away.

"Streak! Get back here!" He pulled his sword and charged, summoning his wizard fire. The sword glowed like starlight. "This will have to do."

Suddenly, Dyphestive twisted out of a dragon's clutches and was on top of it. With the dragon's tail still coiled around his neck, he pounded the dragon in the skull.

The other dragon had a tail with jade-colored scales

and swished it under Grey Cloak's feet, but he jumped high over it and sprinted toward the dragon on Dyphestive's back. He'd learned a great deal about dragon anatomy when he trained as a Sky Rider, and he pierced the dragon with his radiant sword right underneath the wing.

The blade sank through the scales and exploded inside the dragon's flesh. The great dragon bucked and jumped away, freeing Dyphestive's neck.

Dyphestive sucked in a mighty breath and dove for his sword. He rolled to one knee just as the dragons attacked as one. His swing caught the dragon with jade-colored scales in the middle of the neck and separated its horned head from the rest of its body. Flames spat out of the dragon's great maw.

Grey Cloak jumped away from the falling head then watched it bounce once and roll to a stop. He waved his hand and shouted up to his brother, "Well done!"

If Dyphestive heard him, he didn't show it. He was locked in a wrestling match with a black-and-blue-scaled dragon. He head-butted the dragon's horns, and the dragon's powerful legs wobbled. He dropped his sword and put the dragon in a head lock. The dragon squirmed and thrashed. Flames blasted out of its mouth and dropped like burning rain on the surrounding troops.

Grey Cloak surveyed the battleground. It was worse than before. The Monarch Knight and Honor Guard were fighting with newfound inspiration, battling the Black

Guard and the dragons with deadly vigor, but the dragons came down, spitting fire like burning clumps of hail, turning the courtyard to flame and smoke. Soldiers were dying by the dozens.

Zooks! Even a giant Dyphestive in Codd's armor won't be enough. He fished the Figurine of Heroes out of his cloak pocket, set it on the ground, and took a knee. "Make Tatiana wrong one more time," he whispered. "We need you."

In the midst of a burning sea of chaos, he started to mutter the incantation. The ground exploded beneath him, sending him flying off of his feet. He landed flat on his back and rubbed the grit from his eyes. "What was that?"

"That was us," a familiar voice said smugly.

Grey Cloak groaned when he looked up into the sneering face of Dirklen and the bright-eyed and eerie Magnolia. He hated them both. To make matters worse, Dirklen held the Figurine of Heroes. Without hesitation, Dirklen kicked him hard in the ribs. *Horseshoes!*

7

G rey Cloak absorbed two more painful kicks to the ribs before moving into the fetal position.

"Oh look, Magnolia, our old friend Dindae is curled up like a baby," Dirklen gloated. "Imagine that." He kicked Grey Cloak in the back.

"It's not Dindae. It's Grey Cloak," he fired back.

Dirklen tossed his head back and laughed. "Ha! He renamed himself. How convenient." He tapped the figurine on his chin and said, "It makes perfect sense, seeing that you've been hiding for the longest time. I see you even named yourself after a garment. So creative."

Magnolia knelt beside Grey Cloak and brushed his hair from his face. "You have a good eye, brother. It really is him. I'd never forget those handsome eyes. My, how you've grown, Dindae."

Play along. Feign weakness. Then make your move.

"It's so nice to see the both of you. Why, neither one of you has ever looked better," he said as he reached upward. "Ah, I see you've found my statue. Thank you, Dirklen. You were always helpful when you wanted to be." He eyed the dragon and Dyphestive crashing over the grounds. "Now, if you don't mind, I'd like to move on before I'm squished. Great seeing the both of you, though. You look fabulous, all grown up in your armor."

Dirklen stomped on his chest.

"Oof!" Grey Cloak wheezed.

"You aren't going anywhere, worm food." With a haughty expression, Dirklen asked, "Do you really think we would let you go? You are wanted by Black Frost. Oh, how happy he will be to know that we stumbled upon you." He glanced at Dyphestive, who was locked in mortal combat with the dragon Chartus. "Upon both of you."

Grey Cloak offered Magnolia a quick smile. She was staring dead at him with her haunting and probing eyes. She offered no expression.

"What are you talking about, Dirklen? I'm not wanted. All of that fuss was cleared up some time ago. I'd think you would know that, as important as you think you are."

"You still don't know how to bridle that slippery tongue of yours, do you?" Dirklen tossed the figurine up and down. "Tell me, is this of value to you?"

"It's merely a hobby. I've taken up carving since I left

Dark Mountain. I find it very relaxing. You should try it sometime."

Dirklen stomped his chest. "How is this for a hobby? Fool!" Dirklen tried to break off the head of the figurine. His pale cheeks turned rose red. "Augh!" he screamed. "What is this cursed thing made of?"

Magnolia giggled.

Grey Cloak whispered to her, "You get me."

"Oh, you think it's funny, do you?" Dirklen's eyes looked like they'd caught fire. "How is this for funny?" He punted the figurine across the courtyard. It landed thirty feet away and splashed in a fountain.

"Nice distance," Grey Cloak said, "but you could have put more leg into it."

Dirklen kicked him again and again.

"Easy, brother. We want him in one piece; I think," Magnolia said.

Grey Cloak curled up and absorbed more punishment. He didn't know whether it was him or the cloak, but he was holding up well, but he played along. "Please, no more! You're hurting me," he whined.

"Good!" Dirklen said. "I'm going to hurt you. All of you!"

A great shadow hung over all of them. Dyphestive stood twenty feet tall, in the perfect image of Codd in his brilliantly polished armor. He had the dragon on his shoulders. The dragon's head was dangling. He looked down at them and asked in a booming voice, "Dirklen, is this your dragon?"

Dirklen sneered up at Dyphestive and said, "Don't you dare hurt Chartus! I'll kill you if you do!"

"Oh, I'm not going to hurt Chartus. Instead, I'm going to hurt you"—Dyphestive pushed the dragon high over his head—"with him!"

Dirklen started to back away, fear filling his eyes. "What are you doing? Put Chartus down! Put him down now!"

"If you say so." Dyphestive tossed the dragon down at Dirklen.

The dragon's huge body landed on Dirklen as he was diving out of the way. Dirklen escaped just in time, but he was pinned underneath the dragon's tail. His fists hammered the ground. "I'll kill you! I'll kill all of you!"

"Magnolia, if you weren't twins, I'd swear that he wasn't your brother," Grey Cloak said.

She caressed his cheek and said, "You were always so clever, Dindae. I missed that. It was quite entertaining." Her eyes glowed with inner fire. "But family is family." She sent a jolt of energy straight from her fingertips and right into him.

Grey Cloak felt like his head would pop, and bright shards of light exploded behind his eyes. "Aaah!" he cried as a painful tingling sensation raced through the entirety of his body. He rolled across the ground, writhing in pain. He couldn't see anything but bright light. "What did you do to me?"

"That was only a kiss from my wizard fire," she said. "Would you like another one?"

"No, thank you," he moaned with his teeth clattering.

Magnolia dropped his head on the ground and moved away.

Grey Cloak blinked repeatedly, and his vision began to clear. He saw a blurry vision of Magnolia pulling her brother from underneath the dragon's tail. Dyphestive was swarmed by middling fire-breathing dragons, and the rest of his friends were nowhere to be seen, but soldiers battled among the smoke and fire all around. Judging by the pained battle cries and the growing thunder of dragons in the sky, even with a giant-sized Dyphestive, they were losing.

Must move. Need the figurine. He eyed the fountain where the figurine lay and started muttering the mystic words of incantation, but his numb lips struggled with the twisting and enchanted words. *Zooks!*

8

The Black Guard thrust their forces into the courtyard, engaging in battle with the Monarchy's finest. The stalwart troops were terrifying in their crimson tunics over chain-mail armor. A black mountain was embroidered on each of their chests. Their helmets were angular, not rounded, open-faced, with ridge-like spikes on the top.

Reginald the Razor watched the Black Guard and Honor Guard colliding in a ringing clash of steel, and he gripped his swords so tightly that his knuckles were white. He said to Tatiana, "I know that it is my sworn duty to protect you, but I think the side of good could use a hand."

Tatiana gave a deep sigh and said, "No one else is listening to me. Why should you? Go. But don't die."

He was already running when he said, "My gratitude."

He'd watched Jakoby engage the enemy until he was about to burst. The older Monarch Knight had proved to be a fine swordsman, but Razor was out to prove he was better. Armed to the teeth with swords and knives, he attacked with the speed of a viper.

The first two Black Guard didn't see him coming. They were sizeable men, chopping away at the Honor Guard, using bastard swords two-handed. Razor stuck one in the chest and the other in the ribs. The men crumpled to the ground, and he used them like springboards and launched himself at the next ones.

"Here comes the Razor!" he shouted.

Steel rang against steel. *Clang! Bang! Rip! Slice!*

The heavily armored Black Guard were no match against Razor's speed and skill. He parried two sword strikes at the same time and countered and filled their bellies full of steel. He blocked, ducked, cut, and killed over and over again.

The Black Guard fell one after the other, but their superior numbers were closing in.

"Fight!" he shouted. "Fight, Honor Guard. Fight! Fight like Codd!"

Razor's words lifted the Honor Guards' spirits. Using sword and spear, they thrust forward and attacked, pushing the Black Guard back toward the wall. Bodies piled up in heaps of metal, and the tide was turning—until a tide of red-hot flame came from the sky.

The Honor Guard stood their ground, battling and burning. Another wave of dragons flew overhead.

Razor screamed, "Get down!"

"STAY WITH ME, Zora, if you want to live," Tatiana said. She was tucked underneath one of the archway bridges that ran through the gardens. "Or not. No one wants to listen to me regardless."

"No need to be so cynical," Zora said as she watched the horrific battle unfolding. The Honor Guard and Monarch Knights fought valiantly, but even with a giant-sized Dyphestive, she could see that it was only a matter of time before the dragons took over. "There's more Black Guard out there, isn't there?"

Tatiana spoke with a faraway look in her eyes. "Dark Mountain's forces come from the north. They have already overtaken the north bridge that crosses the Outer Ring. That is where the Black Guard are coming from. They fill the city." She sighed. "This is what I tried to warn everyone about. There is no winning. The cause is lost. We have to fight another day."

"What are you going to do? Stand here and watch?" Zora said. "Or fight with your friends?"

"I'm a member of the Wizard Watch. I'll serve my purpose. If I must fight, I will fight, but at the moment, I'm trying to find a way out of this madness that Grey Cloak and Dyphestive have caused."

"You can't blame them for trying to do the right thing. They are following their hearts."

"The heart is full of foolishness. That is a weakness." Tatiana shook her head and looked at Zora. "I'm sorry, dear sister, but I know what I am talking about. The Wizard Watch has seen many outcomes. In almost all of them, we lose."

"Almost all?"

"I'll put it in terms that you will understand. Almost one hundred outcomes to one."

Zora's heart sank. As much as she was caught up in the bravery of Grey Cloak and Dyphestive, she felt the wisdom and truth of Tatiana's words. Judging by the burning and bloody battle scene, she knew it would take a miracle to save them. "What do you want me to do?"

"Don the Scarf of Shadows and find Crane. He has the only means to get all of us out of this." She shook her head as she eyed the dragons in the sky. "But even his wagon can't outrun those dragons."

THE MIDDLING DRAGONS were half as big as the grand dragons Dyphestive had faced, but there were many. Three middlings, saddled with riders firing arrows, had latched onto Dyphestive's legs with teeth and claws.

"Get off me!" Dyphestive said as he kneed a dragon in the snout.

A Risker shot him in the nose with an exploding arrow.

"Ow!" He reached down, yanked the man from the saddle, and flung him over the castle wall and into the moat.

A middling dragon flew into the middle of his back, horns first, and knocked him to his knees. Two more dragons latched on. There were five in all, eating away at his armor, trying to strip it off.

"I've had enough of this!" Dyphestive caught sight of Codd's sword lying on the ground nearby. With a loud groan, he crawled to it. He wrapped his fingers around the handle and fought his way up to stand.

The dragons tried to pull him down like slithering angry vines. Flames shot out of their mouths and burned his skin.

He said through clenched teeth, "Enough!"

With a downward thrust, he skewered a dragon. It let out an ear-splitting scream, and its rider dropped out of the saddle. It was a man with a glowing dragon charm shining on his chest. Dyphestive clubbed the man with the flat of his sword, sending him head over heels into the flower gardens.

Dyphestive took another swing and sheared a dragon's

tail off. He popped another one in the snout with the pommel then stabbed the other two dragons at his feet. Codd's sword cleaved their scales like a hot knife through butter. Its shiny blade burned brighter with each successful attack.

"Yes!" Dyphestive bellowed. "Yes! I'm going to be wearing a dragon-skin vest and boots to dinner tonight!" The great sword struck with dazzling ferocity. Dragon and rider were torn asunder. "Come, sky devils! Come and die!"

Dragons fell like leaves. He killed them in twos and fours. A dozen lay dead at his feet when the Riskers turned their dragons back into the sky.

"Come, cowards! Fight!" he yelled as he slung dragon blood from his sword. His helmet slipped over his eyes, and when he pushed it back up, he felt a falling sensation. The ground and the dead dragons at his feet seemed to be growing. "What?" he muttered. "Oh no, I'm shrinking."

9

Grey Cloak rubbed his eyes. He still had blurry purple spots, but his vision was getting better. He crawled to the fountain and peered into the murky water. "Thunderbolts," he muttered as he stared at all the lily pads resting on top of the green-algae-filled water. Then he looked over his shoulder and saw Dyphestive shrinking foot by foot, second by second. "Thunderbolts!"

He crawled into the decorative fountain and ran his hands along the slimy basin. "Where are you? Where are you? Where are you?"

Dragons passed overhead like great shadows. They covered the sky like small clouds.

"How many of them are there?" he asked as he sloshed through the water on his hands and knees. Inky green water splashed into this mouth. "Ugh!" He spat. "That's nasty. Am I talking to myself? Zooks, I am."

He searched through the fountain's muck and cross-examined his decisions.

Perhaps I should have listened more to Tatiana.

We were going to be dead one way or the other.

There is always a way to escape.

How could I stand by and let Black Frost take this city?

Maybe I should have let the Monarchs surrender.

It's not my fault Dyphestive turned into a giant.

Oh my, there are coins in here. Lots of them! I won't die with my pockets empty.

His eyes swept through the smoke and mayhem. *This is chaos.*

His fingers gently seized a rock-hard object, and he jerked it out of the water. It was the slime-covered Figurine of Heroes. "There you are!"

Grey Cloak set the figurine on the ground. At the moment, no one was paying attention to him. Magnolia was still trying to free Dirklen from underneath the dragon. Dyphestive had started running his way, shaking free of Codd's armor as he did so, but he dragged the shield with him.

"Streak! Streak!" *Where is he?*

The runt dragon had vanished, and Grey Cloak could only imagine that he was hiding. If his little friend was safe, he was all right with that. *I'll find him later—if there is a later.*

With a passing glance, he spied Than, of all people, huddled in the gardens, away from the fighting, kneeling with his scaly hands on Streak. The runt dragon flicked his tongue and appeared to nod at Than.

What in Gapoli is going on over there? "Streak!" Grey Cloak called. "Get over here!"

No sooner did his words part his lips than Dirklen's dragon, Chartus, rose back up, freeing Dirklen, and Magnolia dragged her brother away. The grand dragon set his venomous gaze on Dyphestive, stopping him in his tracks, then it took a deep breath and let its scorching flame out. Dyphestive tucked his body underneath the shield.

Without even thinking, Grey Cloak started muttering the incantation to the Figurine of Heroes. The complicated arcane words twisted his tongue and rolled out of his mouth with a life of their own.

The Figurine of Heroes trembled and started to spew inky-black smoke. Grey Cloak fanned his hand in front of his face. He caught a glimpse of Dyphestive facing Chartus, whose flames had died down. Dyphestive's hair was smoking, and his eyebrows were singed off. Chartus stomped on him, smashing him underneath Codd's shield.

"Nooo!" Grey Cloak screamed. "Nooo!"

10

Under the protection of the Scarf of Shadows's invisibility, Zora weaved her way through the sea of chaos. She jumped over the dead and the living, dodged fireballs dropping from the sky, and ducked under a spear that sailed errantly. *Flaming fences! Nowhere is safe!*

With the bodies of men and dragons violently surging against one another, she dashed for higher ground at the castle wall. She couldn't be certain what Tatiana wanted from Crane, but she heavily suspected that she wanted the services of his magic wagon to haul them out of the grounds of Monarch Castle.

She took the steps four at a time and made it to the castle wall then searched from behind the parapets. Though she saw no sign of Crane, there was bombing and bloodshed everywhere. The rallied forces of the Monarchs had lost their wind, and the swarming dragons were taking them down.

Where are you, Crane? She spun around and looked over the castle moat from between the battlements. The drawbridge was down, and more Black Guard were marching into the city. She followed their approach and watched them pass under the castle's massive portcullis and under the gates. That was when she got her first glimpse of her target. *Crane! What is he doing?*

He was sitting on the wagon bench, eating a green apple, as if nothing else in the world were going on. The weird thing was that no one else paid him any mind. *Crazy Crane!*

She raced back down the steps, sliding by a battling Black Guard and Honor Guard on the way down. After jumping the last flight of steps, she hit the ground running, hoping she could reach Crane and rescue the others in time.

GREY CLOAK WATCHED with wide eyes as Chartus ground his brother into the ground. A chill raced down his spine as a dark-gray fog-like smoke rolled over his shoulders. He turned.

Two figures stood within the figurine's mist, which had started to clear away. They were a man and a woman, both human, wearing deep-blue bodysuits like a second skin. The woman had a serious look on her pretty face, and her straight hair was as dark as a raven's feathers. She held a long and narrow contraption with both hands.

The man beside her was a different story. Handsome, strapping, and rugged, he had waves in his dark-brown hair and stubble on his face, and small mirrors covered his eyes. What looked like metal darts were strapped over his brawny shoulders.

They had belts of strange gear on their hips, and they both wore strange laced-up boots, their chins lifted skyward.

The woman asked in a serious voice, "John, what did you get us into this time?"

"It wasn't me, but I like it," John replied confidently. "Those are dragons." He glanced at Grey Cloak. "Are you an elf?"

"Yes."

"Is this world Titanuus?"

"No, it's Gapoli." He straightened his back and said, "My name is Grey Cloak. I summoned you. I really hope you are on my side. It's been a bad day."

"I'm Smoke. This is my wife, Sid, and I think we're here to help," he said casually as he eyeballed the monstrous dragon Chartus. "You seem all right, Grey Cloak. So tell me, is that one dragon the reason you summoned us?"

"John, this had better not be one of your games. I have to pick little John up from school in an hour," Sid said.

"Text your parents," Smoke said.

"Yeah, I don't see any cell towers around here," she replied.

Grey Cloak eyed the strange contraptions that they were carrying. "I hope those are weapons."

"Oh, they're weapons, all right," Smoke said with a small grin. "This is called an M-60 machine gun. It's sort of like a crossbow or a fancy sling, but bullets are a lot, lot, lot better than arrows or bolts. Sid is carrying a 50-caliber sniper rifle. She's the best shot in the family, so she gets the big gun. So which of these dragons is causing a problem?"

"All of them." He pointed at Chartus and said, "Starting with that one."

Smoke fed a belt of bullets into his weapon and said, "I think we might need the blue tips. Those dragon scales look pretty thick."

"You go blue," Sid said as she put the stock of her weapon against her shoulder and aimed for the sky. "I'll go red."

"Works for me," Smoke said as if he had ice water in his veins. "Hey, Grey Cloak, you might better cover those pointy ears. These fireworks are really loud." He aimed at the spiny ridges of Chartus's back. "Let's make some noise."

Grey Cloak stepped to the side, covered his ears, and took a knee.

The muzzle of Smoke's weapon exploded with fire. Blue bullets streaked through the air. The machine gun roared. *Puppah-puppah-puppah-puppuh!* Brass casings spit out of the machine gun like drops from a waterfall.

Chartus reared like he'd been stung by a humongous hornet. The machine gun bullets ripped a hole through his scales and bones. Erratic flames started to spit from his mouth. He wobbled and teetered on his monster legs.

"Zooks," Grey Cloak said with awe as he watched the grand dragon fall down dead with a *whump*.

Dirklen was on his feet and ran to his dragon, screaming, "No! Nooo!"

Magnolia shot Grey Cloak a bewildered look and eyed the machine-gun-wielding warrior raining down death.

Krak-kow! A sound like a lightning strike made Grey Cloak and Magnolia flinch. The jarring sound was followed by a fiery explosion in the sky. Dragon bits, bones, scales, and pieces rained down. A Risker plummeted to his imminent death.

With one eye closed and the barrel pointed toward the sky, Sid fired her massive sniper rifle again. *Krak-kow!* A red missile rocketed through the air in a glowing streak of fury. The bullet exploded inside the chest of a middling dragon.

"Flaming fences! This is incredible!" Grey Cloak watched in awe as the husband and wife tore the skies to pieces in tandem. Dragons spiraled out of control and dropped like rain. The duo from another dimension stuck it to the evil fiends in the sky.

Krak-kow!

Puppah-puppah-puppah-pappuh!

Puppah-puppah-puppah-pappuh!

Puppah-puppah-puppah-pappuh!

Krak-kow!

Puppah-puppah-puppah-pappuh!

Puppah-puppah-puppah-pappuh!

Krak-kow!

"Grey Cloak, what about the guys in armor?"

"Guys?" he replied. "Oh, the Black Guard in crimson are bad. The rest, in sashes, white, and scale mail, are good."

"John, I need cover! They're diving!" Sid said as the dragons came right at her.

"Makes sense." Smoke whipped the barrel of his machine gun around and unleashed his fury. *Puppah-puppah-puppah-pappuh! Puppah-puppah-puppah-pappuh!*

A middling dragon and its Risker crashed to the ground twenty feet away. Bullets ripped another dragon's wing apart, and the dragon spiraled out of control and crashed into a castle tower.

"Crud! I'm empty!" Smoke said as he dropped to a knee and loaded more bullets. "Stay low, Sid. Those butterflies breathe fire, you know."

Sid fired again. *Krak-kow!*

"They eat fire too!" she said as she watched another dragon explode in the sky. "I'm empty! Cripes!"

Smoke fed his bullets into the chamber and charged a small handle on his weapon. His mirrored eyes landed on Dirklen and Magnolia, who approached with glowing swords in their hands.

Dirklen was frothing at the mouth, and his chest was heaving. "You killed my dragon!" Dirklen said. "Now I'm going to kill both of you!"

11

"What about them? Do you want me to waste them?" Smoke asked of Dirklen and Magnolia.

The words were strange, but Grey Cloak caught the meaning. "Absolutely. Waste them!"

Smoke let out a fiery blast that should have cut the wicked brother and sister down like saplings. Instead, they jumped over ten feet high, and the bullets passed beneath them.

"Leaping lizards, they jump like frogs in that armor. Cool," Smoke said.

Dirklen landed right in front of Smoke and knocked the gun barrel aside. Magnolia dropped in front of Grey Cloak and slashed at him. He ducked underneath the lethal blade and leg-swept her from her feet.

"That's the spirit. Sweep the leg!" Smoke said as he danced away from Dirklen's heavy-handed chops.

Magnolia hopped up from being flat on her back and faced off against Grey Cloak again. "You've come a long way since the last time I saw you."

He pulled his sword. "You have no idea, but lucky for you, I'm happy to accept your surrender."

"Ha!" She thrust.

He parried and counterstruck.

She parried and returned her own strike, which almost took off his nose. "I always liked you. It will be a shame to kill you."

"I wish I could say the same," he said.

They went back and forth, blades clashing, twisting and spinning. Magnolia was really good, but all Riskers were. The fire dancing on her blade seemed to make her quicker. Grey Cloak summoned fire of his own and sent it coursing up his blade.

Her eyes widened, and she said, "I see you can use the wizard fire."

"We call it wizardry," he replied as his quick thrusts forced her to backpedal.

"We who?" she said.

He thought of the Sky Riders. Their loss set his veins on fire. "We! Me!" He hit her sword so hard that he knocked it out of her hands. "Ha!" He put his blade to her neck. "Surrender!"

"Or what? You won't kill me. You aren't a killer," the bright-eyed Magnolia said.

Her eerie gaze drew him in, and he said, "I-I what..." He lost his train of thought.

Magnolia whisked a dagger out of her belt and punched at his belly. He twisted sideways, but the blade cut through his side. Awakening from the haze she'd put on him, he lashed out with his sword.

Magnolia backflipped out of his reach. When she stood up, she lifted her arms and winked. "Goodbye, Grey Garment."

A middling dragon soared over head and took her up in its talons. Wings beating hard against the wind, it took her up and away. She climbed onto the dragon's back and waved goodbye.

Krak-kow! Krak-kow! Sid was on one knee, blasting dragon after dragon out of the sky.

Smoke and Dirklen were fighting, and Dirklen knocked Smoke's weapon out of his hands.

"You are finished now, mirror-eyes!" Dirklen pounced at the rangy warrior and brought his sword down hard.

Smoke slid away from the sword with the ease of a cat. He kicked the overextended Dirklen in the hip and knocked him off balance. At the same time, he pulled two smaller handheld weapons from his hips and pointed them at Dirklen. Dirklen turned and rushed in to attack.

Blam! Blam! Blue bullets blasted out of Smoke's

weapons and pierced Dirklen's armor. Dirklen screeched like a wounded bird of prey.

A grand dragon dove out of the sky and snatched Dirklen up. The dragon's rider was Commander Shaw.

Smoke fired bullets at the huge dragon as it escaped into the sky. He spun his weapons on his fingers, stuffed them back into the holsters, and snatched up his machine gun. "Honey, how are you holding up?"

Krak-kow! "I'll probably go deaf from a lack of hearing protection, but otherwise, I'm fine," Sid said.

The dynamic pair stood back to back and blasted away into the sky. The dragons retreated to the clouds and circled. *Krak-kow!* Sid blasted a dragon from one thousand feet away.

"You're the best, baby," Smoke said as he lowered his barrel and pointed it toward the Black Guard. *Puppah-puppah-puppah-puppuh!*

Smoke shredded the crimson tunics' ranks. As rows of men fell underneath the lethal onslaught, the bullets started to pass through the bewildered men like ghosts.

"What's happening?" Sid asked. Her and Smoke's hard bodies started to fade.

"It appears that the vacation to the dragon land is over," Smoke replied as his body started to vanish. "Bummer." He eyed Grey Cloak. "Summon us back anytime. And if you ever swing by my world, I'll buy you a milkshake."

As fast as the otherworldly warriors had come, they were gone again in a puff of smoke.

Grey Cloak snared the figurine and dropped it into his pocket. The Riskers' forces continued to circle above but from a very long distance. Meanwhile, the soldiers on the ground were still battling for their lives.

A thought snared him. *Dyphestive!*

12

Grey Cloak found Dyphestive lying underneath Codd's shield with his feet stuck out at the bottom. He pried the shield away from the ground and tossed the shield aside. Dyphestive's body was pressed into the ground. His eyes were as big as moons, and his fingers were wiggling.

"Are you well? Are you well?" Grey Cloak shook him.

"Aside from feeling like I was stomped by a dragon, yes," Dyphestive replied with a crooked smile that revealed a split lip. "Is it gone?"

"Dead," Grey Cloak said as he nodded at Chartus. "Can you move?"

"I've been trying to. I feel like I've been stuffed into a coffin that was too small. Dragons are heavy."

"It's a good thing you are as hard as stone." He grabbed

his brother's arm and pulled, rolling him to his side. "Dragons aren't the only things that are heavy."

Dyphestive managed to crawl out of the crevice and sit up with his feet inside. "Whoa, what did I miss? There are dead dragons everywhere."

Grey Cloak patted his cloak and said, "I used the figurine."

"Is that what all of those strange explosions were?"

"That was them."

"Them?"

"Smoke and Sid." Grey Cloak hooked his brother's arm and helped him to his feet. "I'll tell you more about it later."

Dyphestive moved his neck from side to side, cracking it. "I think I can fight." He spun the war mace Thunderash.

"You should be dead. I thought you were dead. I'm glad that you weren't," he said.

"It's good to know that you were worried."

Dyphestive set his eyes on a pair of soldiers that were running his way. It was Beak and Sergeant Tinnison. Their armor was disheveled and their faces scuffed and battle weary.

"What's wrong?" Dyphestive asked.

"It's the Monarchs!" Tinnison said it like it was a curse. "They saw what you did, but they want all of you arrested. Again!" he spit. "But we saw what you did too. You donned Codd's armor. There is no crime in that!"

"We came to warn you," Beak, Adanadel's daughter,

said. Her left shoulder hung out of its socket, and blood was on her armor. "This is insanity."

Dyphestive pointed at a skirmish along the wall. "There is still a battle going on!"

"It's chaos, I tell you," Tinnison said. "The kind that makes you go, 'Augh! Augh! Augh!'"

"The Honor Guard and Monarch Knights are fighting, but they are fighting over who is in charge," Beak said. "The orders on the ground are mixed. The knights fight, inspired by Codd. There is no deterring them. The Monarchs have the Honor Guard's ear, on the other hand. They are being told to stand down."

"But we're winning," Grey Cloak said.

Streak scurried from his garden hiding spot and stopped at his feet.

He picked him up and said, "There you are."

The dragon lifted his eyes skyward. The Riskers were lowering.

"It seems that it's not going to take them very long to get their courage back," Grey Cloak said. Smoke and Sid had taken out at least a score of dragons, but scores more were still left in the sky. He looked at his brother. "At this point, I think we've done all that we can."

"It can't be over yet." Dyphestive jogged over to Codd's helmet, picked it up, and put in on. Then he walked back over to the group. "I don't understand how it works. It won't make me a giant again."

"That's because it's served its purpose," a rough-spoken older man that appeared from the burning gardens said. It was the monarch enchanter, Hyrum. His shoulder-length hair was white and woolen. The robes he wore were pitch black with geometric symbols. He lifted the helmet from Dyphestive's head and tossed it aside. "Now the time has come to move on."

"What? Flee?" Grey Cloak asked.

"The Riskers are descending. The Monarchs do not have your backs. I'm afraid that all of your efforts have been in vain, though I admire them." Hyrum cleared his throat. "Woozah. Too much smoke inhalation. I have to admit, putting all of those dragons down was very impressive. Too bad that figurine's powers are so short-lived." Hyrum shook his fist at the sky. "It sure scared the snot balls out of them!"

A group of yonders flew over them and formed a ring. The bulbous eyeballs with bat wings hovered ten feet over them.

"Look who came to join the celebration," Tinnison said with a sneer in his voice. "I imagine our keisters are cooked now."

Grey Cloak had taken every chance he could think of, but he was all out of ideas. As the Riskers lowered from the sky, it appeared it was all over.

"What do we do, Grey?" Dyphestive asked.

"I'm thinking."

The Riskers and their dragons were lowering one

hundred feet at a time. They would land in moments. In the meantime, the fighting against the Black Guard in the courtyards had come to a stop, but no one surrendered their weapons. It was an organized standoff.

Crane drove his wagon along the wall. Tatiana was under a garden bridge.

Grey Cloak turned to Hyrum, whispered in the old man's ear, and said, "Get my friends out of here. I'll handle this."

Hyrum nodded. In the bat of a lash, he vanished in a twinkle of star dust.

For several moments, Grey Cloak considered running for the drawbridge and hiding in the city, but Dyphestive wouldn't be able to keep up, and he would never leave his brother.

Time was at a standstill while a host of the Honor Guard encircled Grey Cloak and Dyphestive.

Grey Cloak rose on his toes to try to see what was happening beyond the ring of warriors clad in scale mail. Tatiana, aided by Hyrum, jumped into Crane's slow-moving wagon. Razor, Jakoby, and Leena climbed into the back.

Where's Zora?

Crane put his hand on something on the bench, but the hand was noticeably forced away.

Ah, there she is, invisible.

He caught Crane's eye and nodded.

The old fellow turned the wagon away, slowly leading it toward the castle walls and the drawbridge, while Jakoby subtly waved.

Dyphestive moved to stand by Grey Cloak and said, "There goes our ride."

"Let's hope so," he replied.

13

"Crane, turn this wagon around!" Zora demanded. She was still invisible but didn't hesitate to make her presence known vocally. "We aren't leaving them behind."

His puffy cheeks were flushed, and sweat dripped from his temples. "Patience. I can't run roughshod over the Honor Guard, now can I?" He eyed Tatiana, who was sitting in the middle of the wagon. "What is your call?"

The Star of Light glowed softly in the palm of her hand. Her eyebrows were knitted, and she said, "All of this chatter is going to spoil my concealment spell. They see us as one of them." The wagon was cruising through the ranks of soldiers, and no one paid them any notice. They marched right by them with hardly a glance. "Don't interrupt my concentration. We would all do well to follow Grey

Cloak's wish and head out of the main gate before it's too late."

"We can't leave them," Zora said under her breath.

"Do you want to find a noose around your neck again?" Tatiana fired back.

"I know I don't," Crane said, "and I wasn't even on the gallows before."

"No, you were watching," Zora said.

"I was, wasn't I?" Crane eyed the dragons in the sky. "If we move, we need to do it before they land. What is it going to be?"

"Since no one listens to me, I'll be diplomatic and put it to a vote," Tatiana said. "All in favor of escaping with their lives intact, raise their hand." She lifted her arm, but no one else did. Shaking her head, she eyeballed Crane. "What are we waiting for when certain death awaits?"

"You know, I find your grim outlook very charming." With a twinkle in his eyes, Crane grinned. "Lock arms, everyone, and hold tight. It's going to be a hot and bumpy ride." Crane flicked his carriage whip.

Szzz-pop! The whip burst into a tendril of flame and smote Vixen the horse's back. The fire spread down over the horses' bodies and turned them to flames. Vixen transformed from a fine mare to a nightmare breed of horse from the Netherworld. Her eyes burned with flame, and she breathed hot steam out. The fire spread from Vixen's hooves and over the wagon's wheels.

An otherworldly fire glowed in Crane's eyes as he smiled and said, "Onward, Vixen!" He cracked the whip. *Wupash!* "When my wheels are turning, the world is burning! Onward!" *Wupash!* "Onward!"

The flaming wagon turned in the courtyard, scattering the startled soldiers like rats.

Zora hung on for dear life as she felt her eyeballs pulling from her head.

The wagon surged forward at blazing speed, blasting a hole right through the scrambling Black Guard. Double tracks of flames followed behind the wagon as it set everything and every person that it passed on fire.

As the bewildered soldiers turned to see the source of the hellish commotion, their ranks parted quickly, clearing a path to Grey Cloak and Dyphestive, who stood side by side, eagerly awaiting the arrival of their salvation.

A huge grand dragon, the biggest of them all, dropped onto the ground, blocking the clear passage. His skull was decorated with jagged horns of all sizes. His eyes were bright yellow and burned like the sun. The rigid scales covering his body were also bright yellow. His mouth opened, and orange flames spewed out.

Zora's life flashed before her eyes, and she screamed. Vixen turned hard to the left, making Zora's neck whip to one side. She held on to the back of the bench seat for dear life.

The dragon's flames would have engulfed the wagon,

but a shield of mystic energy repelled them. Instead, the fire curled like a cloud above the wagon.

The Star of Light burned bright in the palm of Tatiana's hand. The elven sorceress's eyes were aglow, and her jaw was clenched. "I can only repel the fires so long. Get them!"

Crane blindly drove the wagon through the fire, and they plowed through a regiment of soldiers. "Hang on! I'm going to turn it and make another pass!"

The chaos created an avenue of escape for Grey Cloak and Dyphestive. They sprinted away from the dragon and toward the castle walls.

"There!" Zora said. She pulled down her scarf, revealing herself. "Catch them there!"

Crane cracked the carriage whip, the fiery wheels spun, and the blazing wagon sped after the brothers.

The grand dragon eyed the wagon's path. On its back was a lean, black-haired older warrior. His stern expression showed that he was in command. He made a simple motion with his fingers, and Riskers dropped out of the sky, firing arrows from the backs of fire-spitting dragons. The arrows ricocheted off Tatiana's shield, and the flames rolled over the dome.

"It's getting hot in here!" Razor said.

The wagon was engulfed by the enemy forces. Balls of fire rolled over the wagon. The carriage bumped and jostled over fallen bodies, crushing them.

Zora couldn't see a thing. They were surrounded by flames and dragons. "Where are they?"

"Don't worry. Vixen knows where she is going," Crane stated.

"Hurry!" Tatiana shouted. "I can't hold my shield much longer!"

The wagon sped away from the flames, and a clear view opened up.

"There!" Zora pointed.

Grey Cloak and Dyphestive sprinted down the courtyard roads at an angle that would meet with the wagon. In seconds, their paths would intersect.

"We have them!" Crane said.

Zora stood and waved the brothers on as the wagon slowed. "Jump in! Jump in!"

Grey Cloak raced toward them with Streak cradled in his arms. Razor and Jakoby stretched their arms toward them. Like he had wings on his feet, Grey Cloak leapt into the wagon.

"Slow down. Slow down," Jakoby said, stretching his arms out for Dyphestive.

Razor beckoned with his arm. "Hurry, big fella. Hurry!"

Dyphestive plowed toward them as fast as his thick legs would take him. His fingers had just touched the tips of Jakoby's when a middling dragon plowed right into him and flattened him to the ground.

"Nooo!" Zora screamed.

Grey Cloak grabbed her face, looked her in the eye, and said, "Listen to me! Go! I'll take care of Dyphestive. Go! All of you!"

He jumped out of the wagon, leaving Zora in shock and with tears running down her cheeks as the fire wagon raced toward for the drawbridge. The last thing she saw was Grey Cloak's subtle wave goodbye before he ran for his brother.

"Go, Vixen! Go!"

In a bolt of flame, the wagon sped away, passed under the portcullis, ran across the drawbridge, and destroyed every wicked soldier in its path on the way to freedom.

14

Grey Cloak helped his brother to his feet. "You know, if you weren't so heavy and slow, we might have made it."

Dyphestive dusted the dirt from his chest and said, "I know. You should have gone."

"And let you have all of the fun? Never," Grey Cloak answered as he picked up Streak, who was curled around his feet. He kissed his dragon. "You really should have stayed with the others." He glanced behind him. A path of twin flames burned the ground, starting at the drawbridge. "At least they are safe."

"For now," Dyphestive muttered.

They stood side by side, surrounded by enemies of all sorts: grand dragons, middlings, their riders, the Riskers, and scores of the Black Guard soldiers, who'd made a ring around their leaders.

Foremost was Dirklen and Magnolia's father, the imposing Commander Shaw. He was perched high in the saddle of his grand dragon, Jentak. The dragon's menacing stare could freeze the marrow in an ordinary man's bones.

With Dyphestive at his back, wielding his war mace, and Streak tucked in his arm like a goose, Grey Cloak pointed his sword at Commander Shaw and said, "Are you ready to hear my terms for your surrender?"

Jentak lowered his body to a crouch, eyed Grey Cloak, and ran his black tongue across his giant, razor-sharp teeth. A hot blast from his nostrils steamed Grey Cloak's hair and face.

"Ack!" Grey Cloak said. "Did anyone ever tell you that you have awful dragon breath?"

"Stifle it!" Dirklen screamed.

"Speaking of dragon breath," Grey Cloak said to his brother.

Dyphestive chuckled.

Dirklen and Magnolia were saddled on the back of another grand, which must have been Magnolia's. The grand's thick skin and scales were splashed with pink and white like turtle skin. Dirklen sat behind his sister. He had a leather sling on his arm and was favoring the shoulder that Smoke had shot.

"What are you waiting for, Father? Kill them! Kill them both," Dirklen demanded.

Commander Shaw gave his son a disapproving look. "These are the two that Black Frost is searching for. Are they not? Why would I kill them?'

Dirklen shrank under his father's gaze and whined, "Because they killed my dragon."

"And if you had been more careful, that wouldn't have happened."

"I want him dead!" Dirklen glared at Grey Cloak.

"That is Black Frost's decision, not yours." Commander Shaw turned his attention back to Grey Cloak and Dyphestive. "You would be wise to set aside your weapons at this time. Can't you see that you've cost enough lives already?"

"You are the one costing lives. Not us!" Dyphestive said.

"I'm merely following orders given to me by the ruler of this world. You would be wise to use your talents to do the same." Commander Shaw's tight mouth twitched. "The children of Olgstern Stronghair and Zanna Paydark. I knew your parents. They were the finest of the Sky Riders. I think they would be proud of your effort, even as futile as it may be." His gaze dropped to Streak. "I see you have a runt. How fitting. Now, drop your weapons and surrender. The Monarchs and I have business to attend to."

No matter where Grey Cloak looked, he saw no way out. He considered the figurine, but he didn't think the magic would work again so quickly after he just had used it. *I'll save it for later.*

He dropped his sword and nodded at Dyphestive. "I'm all out of ideas. You?"

"That's not my strong suit." With a heavy sigh, Dyphestive dropped Thunderash. "I hope they don't make me a Doom Rider again."

"I don't think you'll have to worry about that. I imagine that at this juncture, Black Frost has other plans in mind for you—if not agonizing servitude then probably a slow death," Commander Shaw said.

"It sounds to me like you are making a lot of assumptions on Black Frost's behalf. I've heard tell that only a fool would do that," Dyphestive said.

Grey Cloak didn't hide his surprise at his brother's statement. "Clever words from an agile mind. I think I'm rubbing off on you."

The commander climbed down from his dragon and approached. He stood face to face with Dyphestive and gave him a look that could kill. Quietly and with venom, he said, "Drysis was a dear friend of mine. Very dear. I know that you killed her, and I will see to it that you and your friend both suffer for that... greatly."

15

"Black Guard, secure them," Commander Shaw ordered.

Streak squirted out of Grey Cloak's arms.

"Run, Streak! Run!"

The little dragon vanished under Jentak's chest. Jentak curled his head downward, searching for Streak.

"Pay him no mind, Jentak. He is only a runt and, by the looks of him, good for very little," Commander Shaw said. "These are the only two prisoners that I am worried about." He eyed Grey Cloak. "Where is it?"

"Where is what?" Grey Cloak asked as a Black Guard started to tie his hands behind his back.

"The figurine, you fool!" Dirklen shouted. "The one you used to kill my dragon!"

"Yes, the one that you used to kill many dragons—and

Riskers, it seems," Commander Shaw said. "Hand it over."

"I can't do anything of the sort with my hands tied, now can I? And I don't know what you are talking about."

The commander looked away for a moment before he crashed his fist into Grey Cloak's jaw. "Search him."

The soldiers threw Grey Cloak to the ground then removed his sword belt and patted him down with rough hands.

His cheek throbbed. "Easy. I'm ticklish in certain places." He giggled. "Oh, that would be a spot."

One of the Black Guard held him still while the other socked him in the belly.

He doubled over and gave a loud "Ooof!"

"Leave him alone. He doesn't have it anymore," Dyphestive said.

"Don't play me for a fool," Commander Shaw said. "Did you find anything?"

The soldier searching Grey Cloak shook his head and said, "No, Commander. He yields nothing."

Commander Shaw's lip twitched. "I know better. I can see it in his eyes." He pulled a dagger from the sheath on his sword belt and fed a charge of mystic fire into it with his hand. The blade swirled with hot, radiant energy. "Lift him up so that I might have a word with him."

The Black Guard hauled Grey Cloak up to his feet. One of them pulled his head back by the hair.

"I only need to return you to Dark Mountain alive,"

Commander Shaw said and held the point of the dagger under Grey Cloak's eye. "It doesn't matter what condition you are in. Perhaps you would like to keep your eyes in exchange for the figurine?"

"Take his eyes *and* the figurine, Father!" Dirklen said.

The commander cringed at the sound of his son's voice.

With an inward smile, Grey Cloak looked up as he pretended to think. "Hmm... my eyes, which help me to see, for the price of the figurine. I'll tell you what—how about our freedom for this imaginary figurine that you have been talking about? Why, I can whip one up with my fingers right now."

"You are testing my patience," Commander Shaw said.

"Sorry. But that's not what I call a counteroffer. How about the figurine for some beans?"

"I don't have any beans."

"Of course you do. Every man has two of them. They are right there." Grey Cloak kicked Commander Shaw square in the crotch.

The commander's eyes widened, and his knees buckled. His cheeks reddened, and he straightened his back and said through clenched teeth, "I'm going to make you wish you had never been born!"

Jentak gave a strange growl that made Commander Shaw stop in his tracks and look behind him. The grand dragon's head jerked from side to side like he was trying to shake something off.

"What is the matter, Jentak?" Commander Shaw asked, his demeanor suddenly cooled.

Using his hind leg, Jentak scratched behind his ear like a dog.

"Jentak! Stop that!" Commander Shaw said.

The dragon raised his tail and let out an angry roar. Every living person and dragon moved away. Even the Black Guard pulled Grey Cloak and Dyphestive out of harm's way, leaving Commander Shaw facing the dragon alone.

Grey Cloak caught Dyphestive glancing back at him and shrugged. He wasn't sure what was wrong with Jentak, but it was definitely creating a prickly atmosphere. Something in his mind said, *Up here.*

"Huh?" He wondered whether he had actually heard those words. It sounded like a voice in his head, but it was more than that, almost more like a feeling. It was familiar. "Streak?"

"What is it?" Dyphestive asked. His eyes were fixed on Jentak, who looked like he was about to come out of his scales.

Grey Cloak found what he was looking for, and his heart skipped a beat. Streak was nestled between the horns on Jentak's skull like a tick. His eyes locked with Grey Cloak, who realized that he had been communicating in a language Grey Cloak had never heard but understood. "Fellas, you might want to back up."

The Black Guard securing them backed up farther, leaving Commander Shaw and his dragon.

"Jentak, what is the matter with you? Tell me," the commander said.

The dragon let out a groan as if something were eating him from the inside out. His back paw scratched at his head, but it couldn't go any higher, and the tip of his tail flicked at the top of his head to no avail. Suddenly, his yellow eyes rolled up in his head and turned as white as moonlight.

Commander Shaw stepped back, his jaw dropping, when he saw the white-eyed Streak latched on to the top of Jentak's skull. As Jentak glared down at him, he gulped then said, "Jentak, listen to me—"

A torrent of flames spewed from Jentak's mouth and devoured Commander Shaw's flesh instantly.

irklen and Magnolia cried out in horror as they watched their father's flaming body collapse to the ground. A prolonged silence fell over the courtyard, but it didn't last long.

Jentak tore into his brood. With a swipe of his mighty tail, he flattened rows of the Black Guard and sent them tumbling head over heels. He spit another fiery blast at Dirklen and Magnolia. Their dragon jumped out of harm's way and took to the sky. Jentak let out another fiery blast at the Black Guard ranks, turning the men into molten flesh and metal. The Black Guard, the Honor Guard, and the Monarch Knights scrambled to find cover.

With the heat searing his face, Grey Cloak summoned his fire and let his ignited fingertips burn through his bonds. At the same time, his guards fled the scene. *Gah,*

that's hot. I have to stop doing that before I burn my fingers off.
He started blowing on them.

Dyphestive twisted around and head-butted one of his
guards then kneed the other one in the gut. With a grunt,
he tried to snap the ropes that bound him.

"You don't have enough leverage," Grey Cloak said as he
picked up his sword belt. He drew a dagger and cut his
brother's cords. "If it were metal, you probably would have
snapped it."

"I could have broken them." Dyphestive picked up his
war mace and asked, "What is happening?"

"We have been endowed with an incredible blessing,"
he said. "I believe that Streak is controlling that dragon.
Come on."

Dyphestive grabbed his cloak and pulled him back.
"Wait, what are you doing?"

"We are going to ride that dragon."

"I don't think that is a very good idea."

Jentak snaked toward them and lowered his huge head
in front of them.

Grey Cloak felt Streak telling him, *Hurry!* Then he said
to his brother, "We are safe. Trust me."

Dyphestive groaned, but he followed Grey Cloak as he
climbed onto the dragon's skull and made his way back to
the saddle. It was large, made of fine leather, and big
enough for two.

"Now what?"

"Hang on to something," Grey Cloak ordered.

"Are you going to fly him?" Dyphestive asked with widening eyes.

"No, Streak is."

Jentak launched himself into the sky. His huge black wings beat the wind like thunder. In a moment, the wind was tearing at their faces, and they were racing through the sky.

"Woohoo!" Dyphestive bellowed.

Grey Cloak looked back at his brother and asked, "You like flying?"

"I think. Don't you?"

"No, I hate it, actually."

"Weren't you trained to be a Sky Rider?"

"Yes, but it's a long story."

Jentak chased Dirklen and Magnolia. The other Riskers were pursuing but not attacking. They were keeping their distance, and it appeared that they didn't know what to do since Commander Shaw was gone.

A glowing arrow whizzed by Grey Cloak's head. Magnolia had fired it.

"Ah-ha, they want a fight. Well, we can play that game. Can you fire a bow?" he asked Dyphestive.

"Of course. The Doom Riders trained me with every weapon you could imagine." He glanced down at the gear hanging on the dragon's saddle—sheaths filled with arrows, two bows, a quiver of javelins, and spears. He grabbed the bow, loaded an arrow, and pulled back the string. "It's going to be odd shooting at something flying away from us."

"Don't aim for them," he said, pointing at Dirklen and Magnolia. "Aim at them!" He pointed at their pursuers.

Dyphestive let loose an arrow that didn't have a glow on the tip. It zinged through the air and bounced off a dragon's horn. "I don't think these arrows are going to do much good."

As the dragons chased one another through the air, Grey Cloak kept his eyes on Magnolia. Her aim was steady, and she was undeterred even though Jentak was pulling away. She fired, and the glowing arrow sailed true.

Grey Cloak plucked the arrow out of the air. "Ah-ha! Look, I caught it!" He handed it to Dyphestive. "Use this one!"

Magnolia's teeth were clenched, and she shook her fist at him. She turned and said something to her brother.

Dyphestive fired the arrow at the nearest dragon tracking them. The shaft exploded in the dragon's face and caused it to veer away. "Taste the thunder!" He elbowed Dyphestive. "Give me another one of those arrows!"

"I don't have any more. No, wait." He slipped an arrow out of the quiver, summoned his wizardry, and charged it with fire. "Here, use this one." He charged up another and another. "And this one and this one."

Dyphestive fired arrow after arrow. Some hit and some

missed, but the Riskers stayed at bay. None of them were willing to take on Jentak and his deadly riders.

Grey Cloak grinned. He could see the dragon charms on the chests of most of the riders. They weren't naturals like him and Dyphestive. They didn't have the ability to use the wizard fire, as Dirklen and Magnolia liked to call it. Without the dragon charms, most of the Riskers were ordinary by comparison, if not all.

"I think they're scared," Grey Cloak said, though the winds rushed by, drowning out his voice.

"What?" Dyphestive asked.

"They are scared! Look at them. I can see the white in their eyes and their teeth chattering!"

Dyphestive nodded, fired another arrow, and blasted a Risker clear out of the saddle.

Over a score of Riskers still pursued them, but it seemed that the fire had gone out of them.

"Why aren't they attacking?' Dyphestive asked.

"I don't know, but I'm not complaining."

Dirklen and Magnolia's dragon lifted higher and turned north. Jentak pursued, as did the rest of the Riskers. All of them jettisoned high above Monarch City's north bridge and crossed over the Outer Ring.

Jentak drifted away and downward, and his speed slowed. Led by Dirklen and Magnolia, the Riskers soared away north, back toward Dark Mountain.

"I can't believe it!" Grey Cloak said. "They are running!"

Dyphestive put the bow away and said, "I can't believe it either." He looked over the side of the dragon. "What about all of the Black Guard soldiers on the bridge?"

Grey Cloak shrugged, pointed downward, and said, "Streak, we need to finish them!"

Jentak dove toward the great bridge, which was long and very wide. The Black Guard partially filled it. Jentak opened his maw and turned loose his dragon fire. He ran a trail over a hundred yards long right over the heart of the enemy. Burning Black Guard ran screaming and jumped from the great bridge down into the canyon's water below.

The tide had turned. Monarch City was saved.

Jentak aimed for Monarch Castle and did a flyby past the Monarchs, who stood gaping on their terraces. Grey Cloak and Dyphestive waved triumphantly at them.

"I wonder if we will get a reward for saving the city," Grey Cloak said as they circled high above it. "No doubt we should."

"Victory is reward enough for me," Dyphestive said with a grin.

Streak unlatched from Jentak's skull, spread his wings, and drifted in the sky. Jentak's eyes were no longer white but back to normal.

"Streak, you can fly!" The hairs on Grey Cloak's neck rose. He was face to face with Jentak, who'd turned his head around. The dragon's yellow eyes burned like fire.

Grey Cloak reached behind himself and tapped Dyphestive on the shoulder. "Jump."

"What?" Dyphestive asked. He turned, and his eyes grew the moment he saw Jentak's eyes.

"Jump!" Grey Cloak shoved Dyphestive off the dragon's saddle, and they plummeted toward their death.

17

Dyphestive fell backward off the dragon, clawing at the air and screaming, "Grey Cloooak!"

"Hang on!" Grey Cloak said. "Well, you know what I mean." He turned his body downward and dove. Freefalling through the sky, he caught up with his brother and grabbed his arms. "I have you!"

Dyphestive looked past his brother's shoulder and said, "No one has you!"

As they plunged toward the top spires of Monarch Castle, the Cloak of Legends billowed out and gradually slowed their fall, but they were still moving fast.

"Zooks!" Grey Cloak said. By himself, in the cloak, he would fall as softly as a feather, but in with another person, it was different. Dyphestive was three times heavier, if not more. They were still sinking like a stone in water. "This might hurt, brother."

"Might hurt?"

"Well, the glass probably won't hurt, but what's underneath it might."

Looking down, they both screamed. "Aaahhh!"

They crashed right through a stained-glass dome, smashing it into shards of scintillating colors, then landed in a bed of silk pillows. They hit hard in an explosion of feathers. "Oof!"

Women's screams surrounded them.

Grey Cloak had landed on Dyphestive's chest, knocking the wind out of both of them. Even with the pillows, Grey Cloak felt like he'd landed on concrete. When he caught his breath, he groaned, "Thanks for breaking my fall."

"Thanks for slowing us down." Dyphestive sat up like he'd woken from a good night's sleep. He tapped his brother's shoulder. "I think we are dead."

"Why do you say that?" Grey Cloak asked.

"Because we are surrounded by angels."

Grey Cloak's eyes popped open, and he immediately sat up. "Hello."

The plush room was filled with satin feather pillows and beautiful women of all races in silky garments. One woman was as good-looking as the next, with curvy figures and long eyelashes. Some of them seemed frightened, but most of them were alluring and playful.

Grey Cloak swallowed the lump in his throat and stood

up with the help of his brother. He quietly said to him, "I don't think we are dead. I know what this is. It's one of those harems."

Dyphestive tipped his head back and said, "Aaah. That makes sense."

Clearing his throat, Grey Cloak stiffened as a sharp pain lanced through his back, then he grunted as he straightened and cleared his throat again. "Don't be alarmed, ladies. We are not the enemy. As a matter of note, we are, in fact, the very heroes that saved your fair city. Allow me to introduce myself." He gave a small bow. "I am Grey Cloak, and this is Dyphestive... at your service."

The gorgeous women bathed in perfume let out a series of playful giggles.

"I'm very sorry about your glass dome and your pillows," he said as he shook the glass off of one and gently set it down.

Dyphestive did the same and, without taking his big eyes off them, said, "Yes, you have very nice pillows. Sorry that I landed on them."

The harem giggled playfully again, and gradually, a knot of them crept closer until their enticing silks and bodies brushed up against them.

"You can stay. We won't tell," one of them said. Her voice was a purr. She was a dark-eyed beauty with piles of wavy shoulder-length air. "You are so big and handsome. Stay with me. Stay with us forever."

"Forever sounds like a very long time," Grey Cloak said as a blond elf wrapped her arms around his waist. "But I have time. Don't you, Dyphestive?"

"Uh..." Dyphestive responded as more women trapped him with their bodies.

The double entry doors to the plush room burst open, and Monarch Knights spilled inside. The harem girls scattered like rats. The soldiers surrounded the brothers with a ring of spears.

Dyphestive and Grey Cloak lifted their hands.

"I've got a bad feeling that we are right back where we started," Grey Cloak said and winked at one of the girls. "But this view sure is nice."

18

Dyphestive sat against the wall of the dungeon cell—the same cell they'd been imprisoned in hours earlier—whistling a peppy tune. It was the same song over and over again, and it had been going on for over an hour.

Grey Cloak took his fingers out of his ears and asked, "Would you please stop that?"

"Huh? Oh, the whistling," Dyphestive said. "Sorry, sometimes I forget that I'm doing it out loud. You know that."

"Yes, I remember, but it's been a long time since I've heard it."

"It has been a while, hasn't it?"

"Since Havenstock?"

Dyphestive nodded. "I believe so. Times were much simpler back then."

Grey Cloak begrudgingly agreed, but he didn't show it. If there was one thing he didn't miss, it was the back-breaking work he'd done for Rhonna for three long seasons. In retrospect, he had to admit that it had helped shape him into the person he'd become. He wouldn't mind the moon face of that grumpy curmudgeon again. Even an earful from her would be a treat compared to the last life-threatening situations they'd been in.

"Do you think they are going to try to hang us again?" Dyphestive asked.

"They'll probably try something else, like beheading."

Dyphestive rubbed his neck and grimaced. "Always with the neck." A moment afterward, he managed a boyish smile. "Did you get a good look at me in Codd's armor?"

"Did I ever. I'd never seen or imagined the likes of it. You became a giant. How did you know?"

"I can't say, but a feeling overcame me, urging me to put it on. Do you really think that I have Codd's blood in me?"

"Well, you don't look like an ogre, but if you keep growing, you might be as big as one. The truth is that I don't have any idea if that legend about Codd is true or not. After all, it's only a legend."

Dyphestive lifted his shoulders and bobbed his chin. "Thanks for saving me from falling."

"Thanks for the softer landing." He smirked. "I have to admit that we are getting better at not dying."

"It makes me wonder if we can even die at all."

"I've thought the same thing more than once. Look at what we have withstood—an army and an army of dragons. So far, we are doing good."

"Agreed."

Grey Cloak stood and squinted at the dungeon bars. They were alone, aside from two Honor Guards posted outside. They stood on each side of the cell, holding spears. "Excuse me, but could I get something to drink?" he asked.

The guards didn't move from their posts. At the farther end of the hall, a metal door squeaked on its hinges as it opened and closed.

Grey Cloak stuck his nose through the bars. "Dyphestive, it's your friends Beak and Sergeant Tinnison."

Dyphestive rushed over to the cell door and pushed his broad face against the metal. "It *is* them. Over here! Over here!"

"Stifle it, Baby Face. We know you are here. Every soldier in the city knows you are here. No need to announce it," Sergeant Tennison said. His face was battered and bruised, and his hair was a mess. He eyed the other two guards. "You two, dismissed."

"How are you feeling?" Beak asked Dyphestive.

"Me? I'm as well as a well digger."

"A well digger?" She gave him a confused look. "What does that mean?"

"Uh, I don't know." Dyphestive rubbed the back of his head, but he couldn't stop staring at her nose.

Beak had dark rings underneath her eyes, and her dark hair was curled in some places and singed. "My nose is broken."

"Are you sure?" Grey Cloak asked.

Dyphestive elbowed him. "I'm sure it will get better. It looks fine to me."

"If you say so," she said as she gave them both an astonished look that she was trying to hide. "I saw what you both did, but I could hardly believe my eyes. You saved Monarch City."

"Of course we did." Grey Cloak huffed on his fingernails and polished them on his cloak. "I can only assume there is a very, very, very big reward for that."

"Not according to the Monarchs," Tinnison said with disgust. "No sooner had you saved the city than the entire castle became divided. Half of them are elated, while the other half fears Dark Mountain's wrath. I know you did the right thing, and as much as it hurts to say this—because I'm not one to be thankful for anything aside from mead and elk ribs—I'm grateful."

"So am I. You were both very brave and oddly resourceful," Beak admitted.

"What now?" Grey Cloak asked.

Tinnison ran his fingers through his hair. "Hyrum told us to meet him here. I think he's in the middle of sorting out everything that happened. Who knows what might happen? The Monarchs are a bunch of kooks."

Beak gave Tinnison a grave look.

Tinnison shrugged. "I don't care anymore. Not after everything that happened today. Let them feed me to the moat monsters. After today, I should have been dead anyway."

"I hear someone coming," Grey Cloak said.

Everyone turned and looked down the hall.

Hyrum approached. Two yonders hung back behind him.

He nodded at Grey Cloak and Dyphestive and said, "I hope you are well."

"We are *so far*," Grey Cloak answered.

Hyrum had a grave look on his face. "I have news. I am ordered to escort you to the throne room of the Monarch King. Sergeant Tinnison, open the gate, and I will shackle them."

Sergeant Tinnison removed the ring of keys from his belt, opened the door, and said, "It's been nice knowing you both. Now do me one last favor and don't bring my name up."

19

"Do you see that? Do you see that? All of my tiger rosebushes are gone! I've been growing those since I was a boy. Now look at my gardens! They are wiped out!" the human Monarch King said. He was a wizened old man with a sagging face that had jowls that wiggled when he spoke. His robes were golden and glittery with a deep-red trim. A white cape with a leopard-skin collar dragged behind him when he walked. Otherwise, he had nothing extraordinary about him except that he was nearly eight feet tall. "This is a crisis!"

Grey Cloak and Dyphestive exchanged uncertain looks. After Hyrum bound their arms behind their backs with mystic ropes of gleaming fiber, he had brought them to the top of one of Monarch Castle's high towers. It was wider than the rest. From the ground, it was difficult to judge the enormousness of it, but its stone floor was every bit of fifty feet from one side to the other, and a solid-gold throne was in the middle.

The throne wasn't the only thing that was golden either. The Monarch Knights wore gold-plated armor with other weapons and gear to match. They made a ring around the throne, twelve in all, and they were paired with enchanters whose heads were hidden in the hoods of their gold wizard robes.

The Monarch King leaned over the parapet. "Look at the fires. That is dragon fire! I saw the dragons myself, soaring by like buzzing flies." He waved his hand back and forth in aggravation. "It wasn't supposed to happen like this. It wasn't supposed to happen this way at all." He glared down at Hyrum. "Who are these people that have done this?"

Hyrum said, "Your Majesty, let me introduce you to the men that have risked all to save our city. This is Grey Cloak and Dyphestive."

The Monarch King's eyes grew wide. "Saved our city? Does it look like it was saved to you? My gardens are in ruins, my soldiers are dead, and dead dragons are sprawled out everywhere." He clenched his fist in Hyrum's face and said, "None of this would have happened if they had not interfered. I had it all under control. Now this! Look at my tiger rose bushes. Did you see them?"

Grey Cloak scratched his head and said, "Your bushes will grow back."

The Monarch King froze. With his back turned to Grey Cloak, he said, "Who dares to speak without being spoken to? I should have them tossed from the tower."

Please do. I'd be better off.

The lanky old king spun around, locked eyes with Grey Cloak, and said, "What did you say?"

You heard that?

"Yes, I did!" the king said. "You arrogant little rooster. I've lived one hundred years. I've ruled for eighty. I know people. Hear the thoughts in their minds. That is why I am the Monarch King!"

"You are a mad monarch," Grey Cloak said boldly.

Dyphestive nudged him and asked, "What are you doing?"

"Speaking my mind. After all, he can read it." Grey Cloak looked the old Monarch King dead in the eye and said, "You should be thanking us. We saved Monarch City and perhaps you all that are in it as well. And all that you are worried about are your flowers."

"Fool!" The Monarch King's voice cracked. "Look at you, merely a child yet full of boasts."

"Black Frost would destroy your entire kingdom, but you let him in to exert his will. How long did you think that would last?"

"I had a plan. Do you think I've come to live so long

without a plan?" He poked Grey Cloak in the chest with one of his gaudy-jewelry-covered fingers. "I knew Black Frost's plans. I had my own plans. Now you've ruined everything." He grabbed Grey Cloak and Dyphestive by their ears and tugged them along like children then pushed them to the edge of the parapet. "Do you see that?"

They faced the northern bridge. Soldiers were scrambling across the long stretch back toward the city.

"Do you hear that?" the Monarch King asked.

Grey Cloak could clearly hear the sound of hammers striking metal. He nodded.

"That bridge took a decade to build. One decade. And it is ancient, far more ancient than men. Now look at what you have forced me to do."

The northern bridge moved up and down. A terrible sound of metal and stone twisting, popping, and breaking assaulted Grey Cloak's ears. All of a sudden, as if its legs had vanished, the bridge fell into the Outer Rings canyon and crashed with a loud and resounding impact that sounded like the entire city had exploded.

The collapse caused huge waves to flow around the canyon. Smoke and debris rose out of the water-filled expanse.

"Do you mind me asking why you did that?" Grey Cloak said.

"Because you didn't give me a choice, you fool. Monarch City could have lived in peace with Dark Mountain, but thanks to you, now we are officially at war." He gave them both a disappointed look. "The blood of my citizens, my soldiers, is now on your hands. You'd better remember that." The Monarch King turned his back and headed to his throne and sat down. He let out a long sigh.

"Your Majesty, what is your will?" Hyrum asked.

"No doubt Black Frost will want them, but he can't have what I've already killed." He tapped the arm of his golden chair. "Hyrum, you know what to do. See to it that I never see this pair again, ever, for mercy's sake!"

20

It was night, and Zora paced inside Crane's apartment. She wasn't alone. Jakoby and Leena sat on the sofa, while Tatiana and Razor were quietly talking on the balcony. It had been over a day since they had escaped on what Crane liked to call his Wheels of Fire. Since then, they'd seen no signs of Grey Cloak and Dyphestive, or Streak and Than, for that matter.

Tatiana entered the room. Her sheer curtains dusted her shoulder as she passed. "You look worried," she said to Zora. "Why don't you sleep? We will wait."

Zora sat on a stool in the small kitchen and said, "No, I'll wait for Crane to arrive. I'm sure that he'll be back soon."

"Waiting like this isn't going to bring him back any sooner," Tatiana said. "Go rest."

"The more you ask, the less likely I am to do it." Zora yawned. She caught Tatiana's "I told you so" look and said, "Don't say it."

Zora hadn't even napped since they'd made their way safely back to the apartment. From the rooftops, they'd watched the final battle unfold in the sky. With horror, she had watched Grey Cloak and Dyphestive fall from a dragon's back and plummet to their deaths. Her heart had dropped with them, and she shook for hours. Tatiana comforted her the best she could, with soothing words and a shoulder to cry on.

Jakoby did the same. "That was one of the slowest falls that I ever did see," he said. "Something isn't right about that."

All Zora knew was what she'd seen. She couldn't imagine that they'd survived it. In the meantime, the invasion of Dark Mountain had come to an end, and word spread that the Northern Bridge had been dropped into the Outer Ring. The entire city was in shock but thankful.

"How about a cup of coffee?" Razor asked as he stepped into the room. "I make it good and strong."

"All I've done is drink coffee since we came here." Jakoby picked his mug up from the table and handed it to Razor. "And I'll be glad to partake in another pot or two."

Tatiana shared serious looks with Zora.

"We need to discuss what we need to do about Talon. I

can't stay here, and I want you to come with me, Zora. I don't think it will be safe for you here either."

"I'm not going anywhere until I know what happened to them," she responded.

"I wouldn't either," Razor said.

Tatiana shot him a look.

Razor shrugged. "What? It's out of respect." He started to fill a coffee urn with water from an upright cistern that sat on four legs. "Oh no, we have a serious problem."

"What?" Zora asked.

"We are out of water." Razor hefted the empty cistern onto his shoulders and said cheerfully, "No worries, everyone. I'll fetch more from the town drinker." He sauntered over to the door and opened it.

Crane stood outside the door with a long face. Razor stepped back and let him in.

Zora hopped off the stool and rushed over to him. "I see that look in your eye. What's wrong?"

Crane massaged his bulging jowls and said, "I'm sorry. I've been outside for a while, trying to find the words to say."

Everyone in the room was standing, and they surrounded Crane, hanging on his every word.

Zora's heart tumbled. She wished more than anything that the blood brothers were still alive, but she'd seen what she'd seen. With her fingernails digging into her palm, she asked, "Say what, Crane?"

The old man swallowed and, with a shaky voice, said, "I'm sorry to say, but Grey Cloak and Dyphestive are gone."

Zora sank back into Jakoby's arms. Tears started to stream down her face.

"I'm sorry, Zora," Tatiana said as she hugged her. "I understand your pain. We all feel it. Grey Cloak and Dyphestive were very, very brave. If not for them, I feel that none of us would still be here today."

Zora buried her head in Jakoby's chest. She wasn't used to crying. She never cried. Wiping her face, she held back the tears. With a loud sniff, she said, "I guess there is nothing more to do but move on."

"What about the bodies?" Razor asked. "Can we bury them?"

"I didn't see the bodies. I was only told that they were taken care of and it was for the best," Crane said. He placed his hand on Zora's back. "Perhaps it's better this way. I don't think you would want to remember them in a dead state."

"You think that I would rather remember them falling to their deaths?" she asked with her voice cracking. "Do you? I want to be alone!"

She stormed out to the terrace and closed the door behind her. She gripped the railing and stared with teary eyes at the sky. "He can't be gone. He can't be."

A small dragon glided into view with the moon in the background. He flew right at her and landed on the railing.

"Streak?" She sniffed. "Streak, it is you?" She caressed the dragon's head and neck. "Do you know?"

Streak flicked his tongue out and shook his head.

"You understand me?"

The runt dragon nodded.

"Do you know that Grey Cloak is dead?"

Streak shook his head.

"He's dead."

He shook his head again.

A strange rustle caught Zora's ear, and a sliver of ice raced down her spine. Someone or something was huddled in the shadows of the terrace's corner.

Her hand fell to her dagger. She eyed Streak and said quietly, "Be still."

Streak flicked his tongue out.

Zora spun around and said, "Show yourself!"

21

A shadowy figure rose from a crouch. His eyes shone like silver coins in the moonlight.

"Grey Cloak!"

He approached with a broad smile and said, "In the flesh."

"Crane said that you were dead!"

"No, he said I was *gone*." He chuckled and opened his arms. "Aren't you glad to see me?"

She put her dagger away, rushing into his arms, and said softly, "You know I am." Her voice turned hard. "But now I'm going to kill you!" She shoved him off the terrace.

"Zora, nooo!" He fell in slow motion toward the street and made a soft landing on his tiptoes. Looking up at her, he said, "Are you mad at me?"

"Did you think that was funny? Pretending to be dead?" she fired back.

"Well, I did enjoy seeing how much you cared." His fingers found purchase on the stone wall, and he started climbing like a monkey. "I heard how you said, 'I can't believe he's gone.'"

"What? I said, '*they're* gone.'"

"No." He climbed back onto the terrace. "You said *he*."

"Then *he* was Dyphestive, not you. Why would I worry about a trickster like you?" She shoved him. "And why would you jest about being dead?"

"No one said that I was dead. Crane only said that I, or we, were gone. Come now, Zora." He reached for her hands. "Aren't you glad to see me?"

"I should break your teeth out. I was really upset." She took a deep breath and said, "Give me your word that you'll never do anything that stupid again."

"You have my word, Zora." He took her hand and kissed it. "Never again."

She gave him a funny look and replied, "Why did you kiss my hand?" She pulled it away. "Is that how you guarantee a promise?"

"Er... no?"

She wiped the back of her hand on her trousers. "Then why did you do it?"

With his hand on his neck, he cast a nervous glance

about and said, "It was something I picked up in Monarch Castle. A strange custom. I won't do it again." His gaze landed on Streak. "Ah, look who is with us. And he can fly now too." He made his way to his dragon. "Did you see that?"

Zora locked both of her hands on his wrist and pulled him against her body. "I think this is what you meant to do." She gave him a long, passionate, toe-curling kiss.

"Uh..."

She put a finger on his lips. "Don't say anything. Now, where is your better half?"

"I-I, uh..."

A commotion of cheerful voices erupted from inside the apartment.

Zora was the first to reach the terrace doors, and she flung them open.

Dyphestive stood among the group, shaking hands and getting hardy slaps on the back. Everyone inside was jubilant, including Dyphestive, whose smile was as broad as a river. It took a moment before the others realized that Grey Cloak and Zora had entered the room. When they did see them, they rushed over to Grey Cloak.

Jakoby was the first one to shake his hand. "Well done, Grey Cloak! Well done indeed. It's a pleasure to see you standing here in one piece."

"Aye," Razor agreed. "I thought the next time I saw you, I'd be looking at smashed apples."

"This calls for a celebration!" Crane said. "I'll open up my best cabinet of wine!"

Everyone congratulated him in one way or another. The last to speak was Tatiana. She pulled him aside. "You cheated death once again. Congratulations. Everyone but death is happy."

"And you, apparently."

Tatiana raised an eyebrow and said, "Of course I'm happy. Your heroics saved Monarch City for now, but what will you do when Black Frost comes again? Will you gamble with the figurine to everyone's peril? Even with it, it still wasn't enough to defeat the enemy."

"Zooks, Tatiana, I thought we were celebrating, not browbeating." He sat down on the sofa, allowing Streak to crawl into his lap, and petted him. "Go ahead. Get it all out."

She sat down beside him and kept her intense but beautiful eyes fixed on his. "I want you to give me the figurine."

Grey Cloak pulled Streak closer to him. "Why?"

In her rigid tone, she said, "It should be mine, Grey Cloak. It was my love, Dalsay's, and it was given to him by the Wizard Watch. It wasn't created to be used in the hands of the likes of you."

"The likes of me?"

"No offense, but you are a natural. You have abilities

people can only dream of. You need to focus on honing those skills and not relying on the Figurine of Horrors."

"Heroes," he corrected. "I've met those people, and so far, they seem pretty nice."

"Regardless, we think it is best that the figurine be returned to the Wizard Watch. Where it came from." She held out her hand. "Please, Grey Cloak. I promise you. It is for the best."

Tatiana's persistence had his intentions leaning in her favor. Her suggestions were very hypnotic, even comforting. He found himself giving in.

It would be one less thing to worry about. But it's saved us all so many times.

Grey Cloak slid his fingers into his cloak, and he summoned the figurine from one of its pockets. He could feel the faceless features of the head. It was smooth like glass and sculpted into a perfect body. He started to pull it out.

Streak's tail wrapped around his wrist. Warmth flowed through the tail, spreading up his arm and into his head.

Grey Cloak snapped out of his daze, and he caught the look of surprise on Tatiana's face. "You don't want this for the Wizard Watch. You want it for yourself."

"That's not true. Listen to me, Grey Cloak. Please, it must be destroyed."

He shook his head and stuffed the figurine into his

pocket. *I won't let her have it.* "You think that if you destroy the figurine, you can avenge your brothers. Don't you?"

Tatiana stiffened. "It must be destroyed!" Her loud outburst silenced the room.

"I'm going to keep it," he said.

She stood up and said, "It will be to your peril. I promise you."

"I'll take my chances."

Tatiana glared at him, turned around, and stormed out of the room. "Razor, come on!"

Razor guzzled down his wine and grabbed a bottle from the table. He winked at Crane and ran after her, saying, "Coming."

22

The celebration was in full swing when Hyrum de Sol appeared in the room and startled the boots off everyone. The old enchanted eyes sparkled under his helmet of woolen white hair, but there was no mistaking the disappointment in his expression.

"Why so glum, chum?" Crane asked as he offered the enchanter a glass. "Try some underling port. It's the very best."

Hyrum gave him a dumbfounded look and said, "You haven't told them, have you, Crane? If you had, you wouldn't still be here."

"I was getting around to it. Have a drink."

Hyrum took the goblet. "Underling port, eh? Why, the last time I had this, well, I was young, and frankly, I can't remember what happened after the third glass." He took a sip. "My, that is good. If we had time, I'd ask how you came to have it, but we don't have time. Should I fill them in, or will you?"

Crane gave his same open-mouthed, surprised expression, shrugged, and drank.

"What is he talking about?" Zora whispered to Grey Cloak.

"The arrangement," he answered.

"What arrangement?"

"I'll tell you what the conditions of the arrangement are," Hyrum said after he'd finished the port and set the goblet down on the table. "My, that's good. Even the Monarchs can't get their hands on that. By order of the Monarch King, in exchange for your lives, you have been banished from Monarch City, from this moment on—well, actually, *that* moment, until the reign of the Monarch King ends. Any record of your existence will be scrubbed from the annals. It will be as if you never existed. But if you return, under any circumstances whatsoever, and are discovered, you will be sentenced to death. Most likely fed to the moat monsters in the dark of night. The Monarchs do that oftentimes."

"Crane! Why didn't you tell us this?" Zora asked.

"I like Monarch City, and I'm banished too. And what about my apartment, Hyrum? I've paid a year's rent in full. Are you going to retrieve my investment?" Crane asked.

"Don't be foolish. You need to go now. The Monarchs

are watching." Hyrum pointed out the terrace doors. Two yonders were perched on the walls across the street. "Don't try the Monarch's patience. He has shown mercy and prefers to avoid embarrassment."

"Does this include me?" Jakoby asked.

Hyrum closed the patio doors and pulled the curtains closed. "Yes, you, Leena, Crane, Grey Cloak, Dyphestive, Streak, Tatiana, and Reginald the Razor." Hyrum fanned his hands out in a showy fashion. "Is that all?"

"You left out Than, but he is not here," Grey Cloak offered.

"Find him! All of you must be gone in the dark of night, never to return again. Believe me when I say that the Monarch King has shown you favor. Not only that, but he will convince Black Frost that you are dead, giving you a clear path to do whatever it is that you must do. But you must leave now and never come back. Do you understand?"

Everyone nodded.

"What are you waiting for? Pack your belongings and go!" Hyrum ordered.

"I'd be happy to, but go where?" Grey Cloak asked.

"That's not my problem," Hyrum said. "But you'd better be on one of the three great bridges within the hour." He shoved the doors open. "They are watching!" The quirky enchanter took a bow. "On a personal account, I want to thank you." With the wink of an eye, he vanished into a thousand glittery particles.

"I've never lived anywhere else but Arrowwood," Jakoby said with a long look. "I wouldn't have any idea where to go."

"Well, it won't be north. That's for certain," Crane said, slurring his words. His eyes were watery as he staggered around the apartment. "I really like this place. I'll miss my view of the city. My chair on the terrace. Smoking from my dwarven pipe." He dried his eyes on the curtains. "Nothing good ever lasts when evil exists on every path."

Dyphestive had disappeared into his room. He appeared shortly after with a rough sack on his back, his club and the figurine of Codd under his arm. "I'm ready to go."

"'Go where?' is the question," Grey Cloak said. He'd been so caught up in events in Monarch City that he'd never even considered going somewhere else. He'd been waiting for contact from Tatiana all that time, but she was gone. He knew what he had to do, though he didn't like it. "We need to find Tatiana. She'll know where we are needed best."

Jakoby was standing beside Leena. He asked, "What about us?"

"You are more than welcome to come with us and be a part of Talon," Grey Cloak said. "I'd be honored to have a Monarch Knight join us."

"And a monk from the Ministry of Hoods too," Dyphestive added as he cozied up behind Leena.

She elbowed him in the gut. He grinned.

"I'm not a Monarch Knight anymore, but I gladly accept your invitation."

"Good," Grey Cloak said.

Crane blew his nose on the curtain.

Everyone grimaced with disgust.

"Grab your gear, everyone," Grey Cloak said grimly. "We need to find Tatiana."

23

ARROWWOOD

On a rise in the green hills of Arrowwood, over a league away, Talon watched the rising sun shine on Monarch City. From the long distance, the castles spires were starlight-silver teardrops winking in the sun.

Crane sat on his wagon, holding his head and mumbling to himself. "I can't believe we are banished."

Grey Cloak stood on the ground beside Crane. "Is it really so bad? I'd never even been there before."

"Monarch City joins one side of the world with the other. Otherwise, you have to go around." Crane groaned. "I need some water. Does anyone have any water? My tongue feels like it has fur on it."

Dyphestive handed Crane a waterskin and said, "Drink all you want." He gave Crane a hearty pat on the back.

The paunchy, red-faced Crane said, "Oh, don't do that. My stomach is tumbling."

When the company had found Tatiana and Razor, it seemed that Tatiana was expecting them, and they joined up with the minotaur Grunt, who was waiting for them at Eastern Bridge. She told them that they would find better sanctuary in Arrowwood. They rode into the night, by horseback and wagon, and set up camp over a league away from Monarch City.

While the others rested, Grey Cloak patrolled the rolling hills of Arrowwood. The land was rich in woodland and colorful brush that seemed to go on for days. Varmints of all sorts nestled in the trees and scurried over the ground. It was a very suitable climate in which an elf could roam and hunt freely. It was even better when daylight illuminated the land, showing off all the colors and splendors that the wild had to offer.

As Grey Cloak made his way around the camp, helping others pack and rolling up blankets and bedrolls, he caught up with Tatiana. "It was a rough night last night. I say that we bury that hatchet."

She tied her hair back in a ponytail and said, "So long as I don't bring the figurine up again?"

"I'm not parting with it."

"And I'm not going to risk my life, or others', if you insist on using it. Listen, I have to be able to trust you on these missions. I can't do that with so much uncertainty. I'm not going to lie—I hate that object. It is an evil thing."

He loaded a bedroll into the back of the wagon. "For the time being, why don't we change the subject?"

"That suits me."

Grey Cloak eyed the splendid surroundings of the sunny day and said, "Let me guess. You are from Arrowwood?"

"Most elves are, including me." She had a meal bag in one hand and fed her horse with the other. "Arrowwood will give us sanctuary that we desperately need. Not only that, but there are many dragon charms to be found in its forests."

"How many dragon charms do you have?"

"The Wizard Watch won't say. We only retrieve them."

He shook his head. "At some point, we are going to have to use them. But it's going to be a problem if we don't have any dragons. Does the Wizard Watch raise dragons too?"

"No. The Sky Riders do that," she said as she climbed into her saddle.

"But there aren't any Sky Riders."

"There's you and Dyphestive."

Dyphestive tossed him a bedroll, and he dropped it into the wagon.

"First, I failed the Sky Rider course. Second, I have a dragon. And third, Dyphestive has never ridden a dragon or been trained to ride one."

She turned her horse, faced them, and said, "No, but he's a natural, the same as you. We believe that all naturals can ride dragons. If not, we still have the dragon charms."

Dyphestive tilted his head to the side and said, "I can be a Sky Rider?"

"Of course. You are the son of Olgstern Stronghair, a great Sky Rider. Why would you think otherwise?"

Dyphestive scratched behind an ear and said, "I never took the time to think about it." His face lit up. "I could fly a dragon?"

"It's an overrated experience, brother. Trust me," he said.

"You rode on the back of Commander Shaw's dragon, Jentak," Tatiana offered.

"True, but Streak was controlling him," Grey Cloak answered. He hadn't seen Streak all morning, and he scanned the area and spotted his dragon in the shade of a tree. "There you are."

"And we believe that Streak is special and can control many others," she said.

He brushed a strand of hair out of his eye and asked, "Who is we? You speak like there is more than one of you." *It makes me think that you are out of your skull too.* "I don't see anyone else but Grunt and Razor, and I don't get the feeling that they are the decision makers in all of this.

"No, they aren't," she said in her frosty manner. She sat tall in the saddle and carried the beauty of a goddess.

"When I say *we*, I mean the Wizard Watch. I use my arcane powers to communicate back and forth with them."

"It doesn't seem like that is the case."

His neck hairs stood on end, and he drew his sword at the same time Dyphestive lifted his club. "Someone is here! Show yourself!"

A ghostly form in robes appeared between Grey Cloak and Dyphestive, the sun shining through it. Grey Cloak couldn't believe his eyes.

Dyphestive exclaimed, "Dalsay!"

24

Dalsay looked no different from how he'd looked the day he died in Raven Cliff. His brown hair was long and wavy, and his beard was neatly trimmed. His features were strong and handsome, and he still wore the same black-and-gray-checkered, gold-trimmed robes. The only difference was that the light passed right through him, and Grey Cloak could see the landscape on the other side.

Leena sauntered over and passed her hand through him. She jumped back and whipped out her nunchaku.

"Those won't do you any good," Dalsay advised her in his familiar stern voice. "My body exists in this world and another. I'm a shade."

"You aren't dead," Dyphestive said, eyes wide.

"The soul and the spirit live forever, but my body is long gone," Dalsay replied.

Dyphestive's shoulders dropped, and he said, "I'm sorry that you died trying to save me."

"Don't be sorry. Neither you nor anyone else could have done anything about it one way or another. We were over-matched that day, but heroes do what they must do." Dalsay walked over the grass and stood before Dyphestive. "What happened had to happen. Do not feel any guilt about it."

"What about Adanadel?" Jakoby asked.

"You are his brother, aren't you?" Dalsay replied. "He's moved on, but trust me when I say that he is in good spirits."

"And Browning?" Grey Cloak inquired.

"The same." Dalsay's eyes were haunting but bright. "Talon's journey is far from over. In death, the same as life, I am here to aid you. I will see to it that you stay the course and battle the enemy. You have come far. Now, you are seasoned and ready for the next step in your journey, the acquisition of more dragon charms. It is the only way."

"That can't be the only way to defeat Black Frost," Grey Cloak said. "I don't believe it."

"Do you have a better idea?"

"No. But I'll think of something."

"Perhaps you'll confront Black Frost yourself and summon the powers of the Figurine of Heroes and let heroes from another world destroy him. Does that scenario sound familiar?"

Grey Cloak couldn't fight back a guilty look and said, "Yes."

"I thought the same thing, but the figurine is not the answer. It is a tool that you learned to use as a crutch. It will become a fatal mistake. I suggest that you turn it over to Tatiana. That is what I should have done long ago. If I had, perhaps her brothers would still be alive today." Dalsay eyed Grey Cloak. "Think about it."

Grey Cloak tightened his cloak around his chest and eyeballed Tatiana. *Something is not right. This has her stench all over it. She's up to something.*

"We will meet again, across Arrowwood's Great River, in the valleys that have no name. It is a long journey. Be well." With a wave of his hand, he vanished.

Crane teetered in the wagon and said, "I don't know about the rest of you, but I'm seeing and hearing things." He cleaned his ear. "Did the rest of you hear and see a wizard?"

"It's very convenient that Dalsay, after all this time, would mention the figurine," Grey Cloak said to Tatiana.

"I don't take your meaning," she said.

"Do you really expect me to believe that was his ghost?" He shook his head. "Nice try, Tatiana. Do it again, and we are going to separate permanently." He got on his horse. "Take us across the river, and if you want to keep me around, don't mention the figurine again."

GREY CLOAK BROODED for the rest of the day and didn't speak to anyone. Tatiana got under his skin, and he didn't want anything to do with her.

As they crossed the shallow creek and headed over the next rise, Dyphestive caught up with him and asked, "Are you still mad at Tatiana?"

"Mad? Me? Have you ever seen me mad?"

"Oh, you? No, never. Listen, I only wanted to see if you were well. That is all. Are you?"

"I'm alive. We're alive. Why wouldn't I be well?"

"I think you feel guilty about the—"

Grey Cloak shot him a dangerous look.

"I won't say it. So far as I'm concerned, it's yours. You can do what you want with it. Aside from that, is there anything else on your mind?"

"Hmmm... aside from how to destroy Black Frost and save the world, not really. You?"

Dyphestive's stomach groaned. "I could use something to eat. A wild pig and some chicken eggs would go down well right now." He shifted in his saddle. "Do you really not think that was Dalsay?"

"It could have been an illusion. Tatiana would do anything to get *it* back."

Dyphestive nodded. "For a shade, Dalsay appeared genuine to me."

"Who is to say? He's a shade. Can we really trust a spirit from another world? He's not even flesh and blood." Grey Cloak took a backward glance at the others. "I feel that we are wasting our time running around Gapoli, finding dragon charms. We should be doing something else."

"Such as?"

"I don't know. I'm thinking."

"Well, the dragon charms are important, or Black Frost wouldn't want them. I don't see a problem pursuing that."

"Isn't there something else that you would rather pursue?"

"Nothing comes to mind. You?"

"Yes, living on my terms and not someone else's. That's what. Keep this between us, brother, but I feel that they are holding us back."

"What do you mean?"

"We are naturals. They aren't. We can do things that they can't. I'm sorry to say, but I think we would be better off on our own."

"Even Zora?"

"Even Zora," he said sadly. "I don't want her to get hurt."

25

DARK MOUNTAIN

"Dragon's breath," Dirklen cursed, his breath visible in the frosty air. "How many bloody steps are there?"

"A thousand, I've heard," Magnolia answered as she brushed her hair from her eyes.

Since they had returned to Dark Mountain, they had been ostracized from their dragons. The moment they arrived, Black Frost let out a roar so loud that it shook the very rock of Dark Mountain's ridges.

Now, they had been summoned to meet Black Frost face to face, and they had to climb, not fly, all the way to the top of Black Frost's temple, a ziggurat-like structure, wearing their full suits of armor.

The icy wind froze Dirklen's maturing chin whiskers. His fingers and toes were frozen, and the only things burning were his legs. He trudged on, head down, cursing under his breath most of the time, following Magnolia, who'd taken the lead.

His sister looked back at him and said, "Do you think he will kill us for failing?"

"We didn't fail. Father did. But I'd probably kill us."

They were nearing the top, and she started taking two steps at a time. "If he doesn't kill us, what do you think that he wants with us?"

With his usual sneer, he said, "I don't know, Magnolia. Maybe he wants to tell you that your hair looks pretty."

"Is that the best that you can come up with?"

He shoved her in the back and said, "Gum up and go!"

Dirklen had lost his patience long before they were summoned. It had been over a week, and they were banned from flying on dragons. All the Riskers were, per Black Frost's orders. The dragons shunned them and remained in their kennels. In the meantime, the Riskers were put to work doing meaningless military drills and backbreaking tasks. Dirklen and Magnolia had been included in all of this.

Magnolia slowed to a stop several steps from the top and asked, "Are you ready?"

"Of course I'm ready." Dirklen shoved by her and said with a worried look, "Well, come on. I'm sure he would have killed us by now if he wanted." He took the next few steps slowly and peeked over the temple's sprawling platform. He found Black Frost's burning blue gaze locked on his.

"Why do you make me wait?" Black Frost demanded.

The force of his breath sent Dirklen backward, and he started to fall off the steps. Magnolia grabbed his arm and hauled him back up.

He jerked his arm away and marched up the steps to the platform.

Black Frost's monstrous body almost filled the platform from one end to the other. From front horn to tail, he must have been one hundred yards long. Covered in black scales, with splashes of blue on the edges and ridges, he was by far the mightiest dragon, dwarfing all the others that were perched on the temple parapet, facing outward.

Dirklen and Magnolia bowed on hands and knees, trembling.

"Rise," Black Frost commanded.

They complied but kept their eyes on the ground.

"Jentak killed his rider, your father, Commander Shaw. Tell me what you saw."

Dirklen fought the best he could to keep his voice from cracking and said, "A runt dragon latched on to the top of Jentak's skull. Their eyes turned as white as snow. Without warning, Jentak scorched him."

"Scorched Father," Magnolia corrected under her breath.

"It doesn't matter now. He's dead," he fired back.

"What happened after that?" Black Frost asked.

"Majestic one, Jentak chased us," Magnolia said, drawing an angry look from her brother. "We kept our distance, assuming that the runt dragon might be a crypt dragon that could take control of the others. We moved to safety."

"You retreated like cowards!" Black Frost's voice shook the stone platform. "The Dark Mountain does not retreat. Black Frost does not retreat! A lone crypt dragon is not enough to control an army. You failed!"

Dirklen found his courage and argued back, saying, "We lost over twenty dragons and riders! We only regrouped. You called us back!"

Black Frost lowered his head, and his nostrils steamed their faces with hot, rancid breath. "You dare raise your voice to me, flea?" He dragged his paw over and touched Dirklen's chest plate with his claw. "I'll crushed you like a nut and eat you in a single swallow."

Dirklen bit his tongue as he fought the urge to say, "Do it!" Instead, he said something worse. "I don't understand why you didn't level the city yourself the same as you did at Hidemark."

"Who are you to question me?" Black Frost's eyes narrowed. "Your insolent tongue will cost you and your sister." He ran the tip of his claw down Dirklen's left cheek.

Dirklen screamed as if his entire body were on fire. He'd never felt such pain.

Black Frost did the same to Magnolia's right cheek. She fell to her knees, screaming as well.

"This mark is for all to see as a reminder of the price of failure," Black Frost said. "The next punishment will be far worse than this. This is only the beginning. I need leaders of the Riskers that are prepared and strong. The pair of you are not ready, but you will be." He lifted his head and turned away. "Dreadful one, come."

Dirklen couldn't believe his watering eyes, and Magnolia gave a sharp gasp. There was no mistaking the woman walking across the platform toward them. Back from the dead, it was the one and only Drysis the Dreadful.

When she stopped in front of Black Frost, he said, "You failed me in life. Don't fail me in death. Take them."

26

W earing only his trousers, the Doom Rider Scar carried a heavy beam of wood on one shoulder. The muscles of his sweat-slickened body bulged and flexed with every step. He marched right over to the barracks, where Shamrok was waiting with a wooden mallet.

Like Scar, Shamrok had brawny muscles, but damp red hair clung to his shoulders.

They were building onto the barracks where they quartered, and they hadn't been doing anything else since Drysis had died over a year ago. All they did was work and wait.

Scar dropped the beam on the ground. An ax was lying nearby. He grabbed the handle, hefted it onto his shoulder, and brought it down onto the beam with a loud wooden whack.

Together, Scar and Shamrock loaded the beam onto another beam, starting a wall of logs chest high.

Shamrok asked, "What did the dragon say to the sheep?"

Scar didn't answer. He'd tired of Shamrok's musings and phrases months ago.

"Gulp," Shamrok said. He let out a hoarse guffaw. "You really need to loosen your girdle, brother. This won't go on forever."

"It feels like it. It was bad enough that we were shunned before, but now it is even worse without Drysis. At least with her, we mattered." Scar sank the ax into the wood. "Now we're lower than a wagon wheel rut."

"Maybe you, but I'm still floating at the top, if you ask me. It's all a matter of perspective," Shamrok said.

Scar scratched the stubble on his marred face. "I'd think you out of all of us would be more broken, given your relationship with Drysis."

"Women come and go. She moved on, and so will I." His thick red eyebrows knitted. "But if I ever find Dyphestive, I swear I'll end him."

"Not if I end him first." If there was one thing that kept Scar going, it was Dyphestive. He hated the youth more than anything he'd ever known. He'd tried to break Dyphestive, but instead, Dyphestive broke them when he killed their leader. Scar pulled the ax free from the block. "Let's get on with it."

They spent the next few hours notching logs into beams and stacking them ceiling high. As the sun started to fall behind the black rock, they sat down with their backs to the wall and drank from flasks of warm ale.

Ghost walked out of the stables that housed the gourn with a pitchfork in one hand and a plucked chicken in the other. He wore his dye-blue leather skull mask and his full suit of dragon-scale leather armor. His footfalls didn't make a sound as he crossed the grounds.

Scar's eyes followed Ghost until he vanished inside the barracks. "He's a strange one. I don't think I've ever seen him with the mask off."

"Or take a bath. You'd think he'd stink to the heavens." Shamrok's nose twitched. "At least he cooks."

"Yeah..." Scar stood and headed for the stone well on the rise near the outside corral. His boots kicked up dust on is way over. Hand over hand, he lowered the bucket attached to a rope and hauled it up again. Then he doused himself from head to toe with the water. "Ah, that's better."

Scar wiped his shock of black hair out of his eyes and cleaned the water away with his thumbs. When he opened his eyes, he saw Drysis and dropped the bucket. "Kiss my boots!" he cursed.

Drysis was escorted by Dirklen and Magnolia. Imposing, she stood taller than both of them. Her head was bald, her skin pale, and she no longer wore an eyepatch over her left eye. Instead, a blue gemstone eye twinkled inside the socket. The rest of her body was covered in a vest of black dragon-leather armor that she wore like a second skin. She carried no weapons.

Shamrok jumped to his feet and rushed over to her. He slowed to a stop a few feet away, gaping. "Drysis?"

She turned her head, and her cold gaze fell upon him. "Are you glad to see me, Shamrok?" she asked in her distinctive husky voice.

"I've never been gladder to see anyone," Shamrok said. He took a knee and kissed her hand. "I thought you were dead."

Drysis pulled her hand away and said, "I *am* dead. Black Frost resurrected me." She eyed Scar. "I'm not the flesh and blood that you knew."

Scar tried to hold Drysis's iron stare but averted his eyes. She had faint blue veins under the skin on her face and arms. Deep crow's-feet lined her eyes, which were more deeply sunken in their sockets than before. She wasn't the Drysis he knew, even though she looked and sounded much the same. She was an abomination.

"What is with the youths?" Scar asked.

Dirklen stiffened and said, "Watch your tongue, dog!"

"Black Frost sent them here to be trained by us. He feels they are weak and they need to be made stronger."

"I'm not weak," Dirklen stated. "I'll take any one of the Doom Riders apart." He stepped toward Scar. They stood eye to eye, but Scar had a heavier build. "Even though I don't think I can make you look any worse than you already are. I've never seen so much ugly on a face before."

Shamrok let out a hoarse chuckle.

"How old are you, boy?" Scar asked.

"Twenty seasons," Dirklen replied.

Scar nodded. "Twenty seasons, ha. I hope you enjoyed them, because you won't last to twenty-one."

27

ARROWWOOD

Grey Cloak, Zora, and Tatiana hid in the crevices of a rise of rocks that overlooked a river village. Tall, rangy, heavy-shouldered elves wearing nothing but buckskin and furs sauntered through the village. Unlike most elves, their hair was wild, their limbs were thicker, their ears were bigger and longer, and they moved with lumbering grace.

"Are you mad?" Grey Cloak asked Tatiana, but he kept his eyes fixed on the noteworthy elves. "That's a tribe of wild elves. They are practically barbarians. Look at them. If they catch us, they'll rip us apart and eat us."

"They aren't cannibals," Tatiana said. She shifted and got closer to Grey Cloak. "This will be an easy task." She pointed at the village, which consisted of round huts made from stone and clay with straw roofs thatched on the top.

"Do you see the one in the middle? That is the one where they worship. The dragon charm will be in there. All that we need to do is sneak in and grab it."

"We?" he asked. "You mean Zora and me." Grey Cloak eyeballed the broad-chested elves with fascination. He'd never imagined that elves could be so big. They were even bigger than Bowbreaker. "Can't you zap the dragon charm from there to here? Wouldn't that make a lot more sense than our getting killed?"

"You're a natural. You can handle a handful of dull-minded savages, can't you?"

"I can handle them," Zora said, her big green eyes glued to the well-built wild elves' glorious frames. "What is the worst that can happen? They catch me and force me to marry into the family."

"They will make a feast out of you," he said.

"As I said, they aren't cannibals." Tatiana gave him a disappointed look. "I'm surprised you are worried about this one. It will prove much simpler than the others. No monsters, ghosts, or poisonous lizards. You'll be in and out in no time at all."

"I thought we were supposed to cross Great River."

"A little bird alerted me to this opportunity. We'd be fools to pass it up." She shoved him in the back. "Go and get after it. They won't suspect a thing while they are preparing for dinner."

"What do you want me to do? Creep down there in

broad daylight, sneak inside, grab the dragon charm, and run?"

"You're the thief, not me. You'll figure something out," Tatiana said.

Zora's fingers massaged her black scarf. "I'll use the Scarf of Shadows and go in. Tatiana is right. This should be easy. I'll be back in no time." She started to lift the scarf over her nose.

Grey Cloak grabbed her arm and said, "No, wait."

Zora gave him a funny look. "Wait for what?"

He was worried about her, but he didn't have anything else to say, so he said, "Be careful."

She patted his cheek and said, "I will. I'll see you before you see me." She lifted the scarf over her button nose and vanished.

Grey Cloak's gaze followed her footfalls in the grass until any sign of her vanished altogether. The tips of his fingers tingled as he tried to search out the path that she was taking to the hut in the center of the village. There were two wild elves standing outside the entrance, holding spears. Both of them had prominent overbites.

"You care deeply for her, don't you?" Tatiana said.

"Of course I do, which is more than I can say for you."

"That's a frosty statement."

"Sorry, I shouldn't have said that." He crept farther away from Tatiana and higher up on the rocks. "I almost lost her once, and I'd hate to think that would happen again."

One of the barbaric elves' eyes narrowed, and he let out a grunt and lowered his spear. He scanned the area, and the other wild-eyed elf did the same. After several moments, they settled back into their posts.

Grey Cloak's heart jumped, and he started to rise.

Tatiana snagged the hem of his cloak and held him back. "Be patient. Zora can handle this."

"Says you."

"Yes, says me. You need to remember that Zora and I had our fair share of adventures long before you came along. She is very skilled. Don't worry. She won't do anything stupid. She's as wise as a serpent."

He eased back. "You'd better be right."

"Don't let your heart get in the way, Grey Cloak. This is a dangerous business that we engage in. You have to learn to use your head more than your heart."

"That must be easy for you."

She shook her head. "We have to work together, Grey Cloak. And I don't see any reason why you would hold a grudge against me. I'm only trying to protect you and the others."

"If you say so."

Tatiana's jaw clenched.

One part of Grey Cloak liked Tatiana, and the other part didn't. For some reason, the woman, who was so beautiful that men would bow at her feet, got under his skin. Her intentions were good, or so it seemed, but something about her repelled him.

Dusk fell upon the river valley, and the wild elves gathered wood, started fires, and began to cook hunks of meat.

Grey Cloak had been holding his tongue for close to an hour, but the dam finally broke. "She should have been out of there by now."

"Zora is very careful. Have faith in her skill," Tatiana said as she picked her lip. "There is no reason to be alarmed. No one else has entered or come out."

"Maybe it's not in there."

"If that were the case, she would have come back out."

He nodded, but he was tingling all over. He knew Zora well enough to know that she wouldn't dally.

Something's wrong. I know it.

Just as the thought passed his mind, the two elven sentries rushed inside.

I knew it.

28

G rey Cloak stood up and started to jump down the rocks.

"Hold your horses, big fella."

He swung around. Zora was sitting behind him and Tatiana, tossing an egg-sized emerald-green dragon charm up and down in her hand.

"Zora!"

"Were you worried about me?" she asked, beaming with pride.

"Uh... no."

"Really? You look surprised to see me." Zora flipped the dragon charm to Tatiana, who quickly squirrelled it away in her robes.

"Well done, friend." Tatiana glanced at Grey Cloak. "I never had a shred of doubt."

"I didn't either, but it did take you much longer than it would have taken me," he said.

"Ha!" Zora replied. "You wouldn't have made it past the sentries, who are very smelly, by the way. I didn't expect that, seeing how they have an entire river to wash in."

"Savages don't bathe," he replied, smirking.

He looked over his shoulder. The sentries had come back outside the tent and started hollering for help. An enclave of wild elves rushed over on bare feet.

"Still, I believe that your theft has not gone without notice."

Zora hopped over to Grey Cloak and shared a rock with him. "Well, another guard was inside, and I put him to sleep with the Ring of Mist. My, he woke up quickly."

"The wild elves have an extraordinary constitution," Tatiana said as she crept down the rocks. "It's best that we start moving before they sniff us out."

"What are *those* things?" Zora asked with a strong hint of concern.

"Good question," Grey Cloak said as he fixed his stare on a pack of the biggest dogs he'd ever seen. The dogs had flat snouts, blocky faces, and shiny spotted coats. Their legs were long, and they had brawny necks and shoulders. They sniffed the ground. Saliva dripped from their jaws, and they began to bark and howl.

"Those are wolf hounds!" Tatiana said. "Run! We must run!" She took off down the other side of the rocks at a full sprint, leaving Grey Cloak and Zora standing on the rock.

Grey Cloak's eyes followed Tatiana. "She's pretty fast for a sorceress. Are they normally that fast?"

"She's an elf, isn't she?" Zora tugged on his arm. "Goose feathers, they come!"

By the time Grey Cloak glanced back at the village, the hounds were moving their way quickly. A knot of elves trailed after them. "They're fast! Run, Zora!"

But she'd already taken off after Tatiana and vanished into the trees.

"Oh. I suppose I should go."

Grey Cloak leapt from the rocks and landed on the soft ground of the rise. His long strides carried him into the wood line. He slid through the trees like a ghost, the sound of the wolf hounds charging into the forest following him. *They are closing the gap. Zooks!*

He burst through the other side of the wood line and picked up speed, gaining on Zora and Tatiana. Waving his arms, he said, "Go! Go! Go!"

The other members of Talon waited by a large pond, and they had the horses ready. Jakoby led two horses, and Razor led one horse out to meet them.

They raced down the hill and climbed into their saddles just as the pack of wolf hounds raced out of the woods.

Eyes widened, Jakoby said, "Sweet Monarchy! Those

are some big dogs!" He dug his heels into his horse's ribs. "Yah!"

Crane's wagon took the lead on the trail. The wagon wheels rumbled over the dirt and rock. He was hauling Grunt in the back of the wagon. It didn't take long for the other riders to overtake him.

Grey Cloak pulled alongside him and asked, "Can't you go any faster?"

"I have over five hundred pounds of minotaur in the back. Vixen is going as fast as she can go," Crane said.

The wolf hound pack raced after them. Behind the dogs, the wild elves' arms and legs pumped as they sped down the trail, howling, blood in their eyes.

"Turn the wagon into the Wheels of Fire," Grey Cloak suggested.

Crane shook his head. "I can't do that. Enough time hasn't passed. The magic doesn't work like that."

Zooks!

Grunt sat calmly in the back of the wagon with his club across his lap. The bison-faced minotaur stared down the hounds and didn't bat an eye.

What does one say to a minotaur?

Grey Cloak urged his horse ahead and caught up with the rest of the group. "Dyphestive, we have a problem."

Dyphestive looked over his shoulder and said, "I can see that. Are those elves really wild?"

"Yes! They are going to catch Crane. He's too slow, hauling Grunt behind him."

"Those elves are big. There must be scores of them," Dyphestive said.

"I think it's every wild-eyed savage in the village!"

Tatiana's ponytail flew behind her like a banner.

He caught up with her and said, "Give me the charm!"

"No!" she said.

"Look at them. They are going to kill us!"

"There is no turning back now. They will kill us either way!"

Grey Cloak's brow knitted, and he said, "Give me the dragon charm, or I will use the figurine."

"You wouldn't dare!"

"You aren't giving me a choice!"

Tatiana fished the dragon charm out of her robes and stuffed it into his hand. "You'll regret this."

"No, I won't." He slowed until he was at the back of the group and held the dragon charm up high so that all could see. Its emerald facets twinkled in the last light of the day. He hurled it at the elves. "Here, take it!"

The dragon charm tumbled through the air and landed right in the midst of the wild elves. The wild-eyed elven savages' fast footfalls did not slow. With fire in their eyes and crude weapons in their hands, they charged on.

Grey Cloak swallowed. *Oh no, Tatiana was right! I'll never live this down! Zooks!*

29

"Crane, are you certain that you can't turn your wagon into fire?" Grey Cloak asked.

"I've tried," Crane responded with a flick of his carriage whip. "Believe me, I've tried!" He glanced behind him. "They're going to rip us apart, aren't they?"

"I think so!" At the moment, Grey Cloak was all out of ideas. The only choice was to fight, but in the back of his mind, he knew it wasn't fair. After all, they'd stolen from the savages. They had a right to be angry. On the other hand, perhaps the wild elves were an evil pack of raiders. It was difficult to tell, but they were the scariest knot of men he'd ever seen.

"Log!" Dyphestive screamed. "Log!"

The horse riders in front leapt over a tree that had fallen over the path.

"Oh no," Crane said.

Vixen jumped over the tree, but the wagon wheels burst right into it. The wagon bounced off the ground, rolled over on its side, and crashed but not before Crane and Grunt jumped clear.

Grey Cloak pulled his horse to a halt and drew his sword. The wolf hounds bounded toward Grunt, who shielded Crane with his towering frame. Grunt swung his unique club into two of them, cracking their ribs and sending them flying backward. The dogs bit and chewed on Grunt's mighty limbs. He beat them with up-and-down strokes with the blunt side of his club.

Dyphestive, Jakoby, Razor, and Leena charged the elven ranks on horseback, their weapons primed to strike. They thundered right by Grey Cloak, straight toward the angry throng.

We are going to get slaughtered. There are too many of them. Grey Cloak reached for the figurine inside his cloak.

When they were yards from a flesh-and-bone collision, an eardrum-shattering roar sounded. The horses reared, and the wolf hounds cowered and backed away. The savage elves crouched, and some scattered. Many jabbed their weapons toward the sky, faces full of fear.

"*Roooaaarrr!*"

The monstrous sound was so loud that Grey Cloak wasn't alone in covering his ears. The roar shook the air like a blast of thunder and turned his stomach into jelly. He lifted his eyes to the sky.

A dragon soared through the air with its wings spread wide. A blast of fire spewed from its mouth, lighting up the darkening sky.

The wide-eyed wild elves and wolf hounds ran as fast as their feet and paws would take them. They disappeared into the woodland, big bodies rustling through the branches.

The company fought to control their horses as one final roar carried across the river valley. Everyone's eyes were fixed upward and locked on the dragon. Slowly, it descended and landed in the company's midst.

Grey Cloak couldn't believe his eyes. He slid out of the saddle. "Streak! Did you do that?" He rushed over and picked up his dragon and let Streak lick his face.

The ashen and sweaty faces of the members of Talon regained their color, and warm smiles crossed their faces.

Dyphestive was the first to comment. "That little dragon made that much noise?"

"Apparently so," Grey Cloak said while holding Streak out like a baby. "You're full of surprises, aren't you?"

Streak shrugged his wings.

Zora giggled. "And full of personality," she said.

Everyone from Dyphestive to Leena passed by and patted Streak on the head.

"The little dragon bailed us out again," Tatiana

commented. "His timing couldn't have been better. The wild elves are very superstitious people, and that tribe must have had a great fear of dragons."

"Or very loud noises. Wait." He handed Streak to Dyphestive. "The dragon charm!" He sprinted down the trail and stopped at the spot where the dragon charm had landed. He took a knee, and his fingers clawed at the dirt and grass. The dragon charm had been trampled into the soft ground underneath a clump of grass. He dug it out and rubbed the dirt off. He held it up high and jogged back. "Found it."

"Well done," Tatiana said. "I told you that it wouldn't make a difference."

Grey Cloak turned his back and walked away.

Crane worked on freeing Vixen from her harness. His stubby fingers struggled to unbuckle the bit and bridle from her mouth. The horse was lathered up and whinnying. "She's upset."

"Is she hurt?" Grey Cloak asked.

"No. It wasn't the wreck. I think your little dragon scared the manure out of her." Crane petted the dragon's neck. "If you smell something funny, it's because Streak scared the manure out of me too."

With Grey Cloak's help, Crane freed Vixen from her harness, and the horse trotted off.

Dyphestive and Grunt tipped the wagon over as easily as if they were rolling a log in water. Grunt gave Dyphestive a nod and a grunt.

The company made small repairs to the wagon wheels' busted spokes then gathered and strapped down their scattered gear.

"Night has fallen," Crane said with a peek at the starry sky. "We might as well make camp. What do you think?"

"It sounds good to me," Grey Cloak said.

"We will make camp," Tatiana said in a loud and distinct voice, "and leave before first light."

Grey Cloak rolled his eyes and noticed Razor standing apart from the group, staring down the path in the direction they'd come. Fearing the wild elves' return, he said, "We are going to need a lookout in case they return."

"They won't," Tatiana assured the group.

"How do you know that?" he asked.

"I know. Trust me," she said.

"Well, those elves might not be coming back this way, but someone is." Razor pointed down the path.

A figure wearing a full cloak and heavy armor approached, a sword strapped to their back.

Razor drew his sword. "Not to worry. I'll check it out."

30

Before Razor made it within ten feet of the stranger, a shock of blue energy shot out of the newcomer's fingers. Razor dropped his sword and fell to his knees, the hairs of his head standing on end. His teeth clacked together as the stranger walked right past him.

The members of Talon formed a wall on the path and stood armed and ready.

Jakoby pointed his sword at the oncoming stranger and said, "Show yourself!"

Something about the stranger's gait caught Grey Cloak's eye as he moved forward. He tilted his head and asked, "Anya?"

The stranger pulled back their hood, revealing Anya's stern expression but lovely face. She had a white scar on her neck, partially covered by her lustrous auburn hair. She gave a slight smile and said, "Glad you remember me."

Before Grey Cloak realized that his feet were moving, he wrapped her in a warm embrace. "I was told that you were dead!"

Anya stood with her arms hanging stiffly, and without so much as a pat on the back, she said, "You were told wrong."

Grey Cloak broke off the hug and swung his gaze toward Tatiana. "You told me that all of them were dead."

"I was only passing along what was given to me. No one in the Wizard Watch believed that any of them survived." Tatiana came forward with a welcoming smile on her face. "This is an unexpected blessing. Welcome, Anya."

Brimming with fire, Anya said, "Welcome yourself, witch of the Watch, and back away from me."

Tatiana stepped back with a shocked look on her face.

Before they exchanged another word, Dyphestive got ahold of Anya's waist, picked her up like a child, and spun her around. "Anya, it is so very good to see you! I thought you were gone too!"

Anya patted him on the head. "It's good to see you, too, Dyphestive. Will you please set me down so I don't have to jolt you?"

Razor lumbered up the path, using his sword like a cane, and asked, "Is that what you call that kiss you gave me? Oh my, look at you. You are something else, Fiery Red. You can give me a jolt anytime."

Anya looked Razor up and down with disdain. "Who is this lackey? And will you put me down, Dyphestive?"

"Oh, sorry." He set her on her feet.

"I'm Reginald the Razor, the finest swordsman in all the land." He took a bow, swayed, and shook his head quickly. "I'm still tingly from the kiss you gave me."

"It wasn't a kiss," Anya said.

Jakoby stepped forward with a broad smile on his face. "And he's not the finest swordsman either. I'm Jakoby, a former Monarch Knight. It's an honor to meet you, Sky Rider." He took her by the hand and kissed it. "My sword is yours if you ever need it."

"Not likely," she said as she tugged her hand out of Jakoby's bearish grip.

"Anya, where have you been?" Dyphestive asked. "We missed you."

Leena kicked him in the back of the leg and dropped him down to one knee.

"What did you do that for?"

With a frown that looked more like a weapon, Leena grabbed him by the ear and pulled him away from the company.

"See you later, Anya? I hope," Dyphestive said.

With an eyebrow raised, Anya asked Grey Cloak, "Is Dyphestive spoken for?"

"'Spoken for' is a funny phrase," he replied then introduced the others. "That's Leena, an outcast from the Ministry of Hoods. Zora. And you remember Crane, of course."

She nodded.

"And that's Grunt, a minotaur from Sulter Slay," he added.

"Yes, I know where minotaurs come from." Anya grabbed his wrist and said, "I need to speak to you privately. No offense, everyone, but I didn't come all this way to meet you. I have business with this one."

Before Grey Cloak could get another word in, Anya dragged him off, out of sight and earshot of the others. They stood inside a grove of dogwood trees whose pink-and-white petals were blooming.

"What is going on, Anya? Whatever you tell me, you can tell them."

"Even the witch from the Wizard Watch?"

"Well, maybe not," he admitted.

She looked him dead in the eye and said, "All the Sky Riders are gone except for us. You need to come with me, Grey Cloak. We have to rebuild the Sky Riders."

He rolled his eyes and said, "Not this again." He checked the sky. "Are you and Cinder going to kidnap me again?"

"Cinder is not here."

Grey Cloak paled. "I'm sorry."

"No, he's not dead. But I couldn't risk him flying here and the Riskers discovering him or me. I had to hunt you down alone."

Streak snaked through the grass and stopped at Anya's feet with his tail slowly waving back and forth.

She picked him up, cradled him in her arms, and said, "Look at how big you have gotten, Streak. And you are as handsome as ever."

Streak licked her cheek.

She kissed his nose and said, "That was a fine job that you did on Jentak, little one."

"You saw that?"

"I was in the city, trying to track you down, when the invasion occurred," she said. "It was a very surprising turn of events. Well done, Sky Rider."

"I'm not a Sky Rider," he said.

"Of course you are. You are a natural, the son of Zanna Paydark. That is what you are meant to be."

He gave her a doubtful look and asked, "What are we going to do, Anya? Do you think that you, me, Streak, and Cinder are going to stop Black Frost? You saw how many Riskers he had, and that probably wasn't all of them. We need help. Tatiana might not be the best leader, but finding the dragon charms is the only way."

Anya stepped toe to toe and eye to eye with him and said, "She is a part of the Wizard Watch. You can't trust them."

31

A small campfire made of broken branches and twigs surrounded by a ring of rocks crackled at Grey Cloak's feet. He, like the others of the company, sat captivated by the full-blown argument that Anya and Tatiana— standing at opposite ends of the fire—were engaged in.

Anya's fists were balled up at her sides, like she was going to punch Tatiana's teeth out. Tatiana kept her nose up and talked back calmly but with all-knowing smugness. No one in the group dared say a word for fear of having their tongues ripped out.

"Have you ever seen a dragon charm after you turned it over to the Wizard Watch?" Anya argued. "Have you? *Have* you?"

"I don't need to see. I only need to do my duty. You should do your duty as well," Tatiana replied.

"That is the problem with mages. They think they know it all. How do you know that they aren't giving the dragon charms to Black Frost?"

Tatiana brushed it off with a flip of her hand. "They would never do that."

"No, because they never do anything but interfere!" Anya poked her finger across the fire. "What do they do but sit in the towers, supposedly guardians of peace, yet where were they when Black Frost attacked my people? Nowhere!"

"We didn't know where you were," Tatiana said.

"Say the ones that presume to know everything. A funny thing, Tatiana—if the Wizard Watch is gathering stones to rebuild the Sky Riders' dragon forces, then where are they? Hmm? Because the Sky Riders never saw a single one of what you say you recovered."

All eyes fell on Tatiana. She appeared to shrink inside her robes. She had nothing to say. Anya rambled on, keeping the full attention of the quiet audience.

Dyphestive and Razor had Grey Cloak walled in by the fire.

Razor nudged him and said quietly, "I like Fiery Red. She makes me feel prickly and warm all over. She's not spoken for, is she?"

A twinge of jealousy made Grey Cloak's gut flip, and he said, "You might want to talk to Dyphestive. He says that he is going to marry her."

"I did?" He scratched his head. "Oh, I did, didn't I."

Leena, who was sitting beside Dyphestive, threw an elbow into his ribs.

"Will you stop that? I was a stripling back then," Dyphestive said as he covered his ribs with his hands.

Razor grinned. "It looks like the big one has the sort of women problems I'd like to have. Good for him. I have to admit, I like these women. All of them. They have the fire that I admire. And look at the bottom on Red. It's as round as an apple."

Anya stopped midsentence, turned, and glared at Razor. Her fingertips sparked with blue fire.

Razor lifted his hands and said, "Jolt me, please."

Anya's eyes burned a hole in him.

Grey Cloak said, "Perhaps it is time to take a break from this conversation. After all, it is going nowhere." He stood up and ruffled his cloak. "Simply put, the two of you don't like each other. My suggestion is that you avoid all conversation whatsoever."

"Yes, not fighting. Where I come from, the women wrestle when they disagree," Razor offered.

"Hear! Hear!" Crane said and sucked on a wineskin.

"I agree," Jakoby said. "It's the best way to let out your anger and bond."

"No one is going to be bonding with anyone," Tatiana said.

"You foolish men. Shame on your hearts," Anya replied.

"Do you really want to see me break this woman into pieces?"

"Excuse me?" Tatiana crossed the fire and bumped chests with Anya. "I'm not scared of you."

Anya seized Tatiana's arm and hip-checked her hard to the ground. In the wink of an eye, she had Tatiana's face in the dirt and her arm twisted behind her back. "Don't ever touch me again, witch!"

Tatiana's eyes glowed white hot. A pulse of white energy shot out of her body and into Anya.

Gritting her teeth, Anya held on to Tatiana. With pain in her voice she said, "It will take more than that to shake me!" She yanked Tatiana's arm backward.

"Aaauuugh!" The fire in Tatiana's bright eyes cooled as beads of sweat built up on her forehead. "Let me go, you brute," she demanded.

"I'll let you up when I'm bloody ready!" She cranked up the pressure, and Tatiana started to kick.

"Enough!" Zora came out of nowhere, plowed into Anya, and drove her to the ground.

They rolled over the grass once before Anya took command on top and held a dagger to Zora's throat. Her chin lifted when her eyes dropped on the small blade that Zora held to her throat as well.

"Ladies, please, drop your blades," came a ghostly voice.

Grey Cloak followed the women's eyes to the shade of Dalsay.

32

Anya lowered her weapon, as did Zora, then Anya helped Zora to her feet and put her dagger in her sheath with a click. She stared down Dalsay and said, as though she'd seen a thousand ghosts before, "Who is this shade? Another trickster from the Wizard Watch?"

"The truth is," Dalsay said, his stern expression making his transparent form appear as real as ever, "that neither I nor Tatiana can say for certain what the Wizard Watch is doing with the dragon charms."

"That's a fat lot of help," Anya said. "And it confirms what I have been saying all along. They can't be trusted. Grey Cloak, you need to come with me and distance yourself from this pack of deceivers."

"Pardon me?" Jakoby stood and said, "Save your javelins for the mages, but don't insult me."

"Or the rest of us," Zora said.

Dyphestive rose. "Grey Cloak won't be going anywhere. Not without me. And we are staying with Talon. We are Talon."

"Son of Olgstern Stronghair, you are a natural, like us, and more than welcome to come along, but the rest will have to go it alone. They cannot fly the dragons," Anya said.

"What dragons?" Grey Cloak asked. "I thought only Cinder was left. Where is he, anyway?"

Anya stiffened and said, "His location is my business, and I won't be revealing it in front of these snakes. As for the others, we will find them."

Zora took a spot beside Grey Cloak and said, "You spent a season with her. I feel sorry for you. But if you must go, I'll understand and support you."

Tatiana brushed off her robes and stood by Dalsay. "This is outrageous. We were on course before you came along. You have brought only chaos."

"Says the enchantress that led them to the wild elf savages. If not for a *dragon*, all of you might have been dead," Anya stated. Her jaw clenched. "But I would have saved you."

"Such arrogance!" Tatiana said.

"I think I could have handled them myself," Razor said as he spun a dagger through his fingers. "If not for the dragon, I'd be wearing a necklace of pointed ears right now."

"Ew," Zora said.

He gave her a wink and replied. "Too much?"

Dalsay lifted his hands and said in a commanding voice, "Listen to me, please. We won't solve our situation by arguing. Tatiana, my dearest, Anya's concerns are not without foundation."

Tatiana's jaw dropped, and she crossed her arms.

Dalsay continued, "Hear me out. I have a strong sense that some of the Wizard Watch are misaligned, though I cannot prove this. I can only say that I have more questions than answers. With that said, I have full faith that the dragon charms are a vital ingredient in engineering Black Frost's defeat. Otherwise, he would not pursue them. As of now, I do what is expected of me, and Tatiana executes what is expected of her. We have no reason to do otherwise."

"Otherwise. Otherwise." Anya paced, a scowl on her face. "You said that you don't trust them. Still, you serve them like slaves."

"I only stated that I have my concerns. This is why Tatiana and I believe it is imperative that you journey to the Wizard Watch tower of Arrowwood across Great River. Perhaps there, more answers to your questions will be revealed. You must ask."

Anya tossed her head back and laughed. "Ask them whatever you want, and they will tell you what you want to hear. The wizardly ones are only using you to serve their agenda. Can't you see that?"

Grey Cloak replied, "You're right. We've recovered the dragon charms, and for what? No one aside from the Sky Riders and us has done anything to fight Black Frost. And what we have done, we have done without dragon charms. Perhaps we are only chasing our tails."

"So you will come with me?" Anya asked.

He shook his head. "No. I'm sorry, Anya, but I'm not going to leave my friends. We are all that we have, and we need to stay together. If anything, I say that you should stay with us."

"Are you mad? I didn't come all this way to join your group. I'm a Sky Rider," she said with her chin lifted high. "And so are you."

"They banished me, remember? You helped me escape."

"I know, but that was different. You are the only one with the training and a dragon. And you are the son of Zanna Paydark. The Sky Riders need you."

"The Sky Riders need me?" He touched his chest and pointed at her. "Or you need me?"

"You know what I mean. Who is it going to be? Us or them?"

"I told you, Anya, I'm not leaving my friends. You're my friend, too, and you should come with us."

Anya walked over to him, put a hand on his shoulder,

and said right in his ear, "You're making a mistake." Without another word, she moved away from the campfire and strode into the night.

He called after her. "Anya, wait. Come back."

"Should I go after her?" Dyphestive asked.

"No, let her go," Grey Cloak answered, defeat in his voice. His heart sank as he watched her go. She'd come all that way for him and forced him to choose. "I made the right choice. Don't you think?"

"You made the same choice that I would have made. You chose your closest friends."

Razor joined them, slapped his hand on Grey Cloak's shoulder, and said, "You spurned your first woman. Well done. It will come back to bite you in the behind when you least expect it."

33

DARK MOUNTAIN

irklen waddled into the stables with Magnolia trailing behind him. His hand was braced against his lower back, which felt as if it was on fire. From dawn to dusk, they hadn't stopped doing one back-breaking chore after the other, all under the watchful eye of the Doom Riders.

Magnolia collapsed onto a bale of hay. She groaned and said, "My armor is chafing me all over. What did we do to deserve this?"

"Nothing." With a scowl, he started loosening the buckles of his breastplate. He removed it and slung it into the stable's back wall. "Nothing at all. We are naturals, and we shouldn't be taking direction from the likes of them."

"Quit crying, boy," Scar said.

Dirklen's back straightened, and his eyes grew bigger.

Scar stood at the entrance of the stable, which had become their quarters for the duration of their stay. He put a wooden bucket full of water and a platter of boiled potatoes and raw carrots on the floor. "Enjoy your dinner, children."

"Call me a child again, and I'll stuff those carrots into your earhole."

Scar let out a rugged laugh. "Huh-huh-huh-huh. Anytime, boy."

With her knees drawn to her chest like a child, Magnolia said, "We want to see our mother. Adalia. Does she even know where we are?"

"Drysis is your mother now. That is all that you need to know." Scar closed them inside. "Sweet dreams, children. Huh-huh-huh. Sweet dreams."

"I hate him," Dirklen said as he stripped off his sweat-soaked jerkin and slung it over the stable's wall. He was as fit as a young man could be and had a pattern of bumps and bruises on his back and chest. He picked up the tray and set it down between them. "I hate all of them. I hate everything."

"We are being treated like animals." She sniffed. "It's not fair."

"Don't you dare snivel, sister." He picked out a potato and bit into it. "Do you understand me? We'll get through this charade and be riding on a dragon's back in no time."

He tossed her a spud. "Now, eat and keep your strength up. We will not give these snake bellies the satisfaction."

"I know," she said. "But we've never trained so hard before."

Dirklen's scowl never left his face as he said, "I know. Father protected us. Thanks to him, Black Frost thinks that we are weak."

"You can't blame Father!"

"Oh, but I can. He's the reason we are here!" His voice started to crack. "If he hadn't died, we wouldn't be here." He slung a potato, and it splattered against the wall. "It's his fault!"

Magnolia rocked back and forth and said, "We are spoiled, aren't we?"

Dirklen picked up a raw carrot and started eating. "It doesn't matter. We are what we are, and we need to be prepared to fill Father's boots before someone else does." He spit out the rough end of the carrot. "He should have prepared us for this."

"I think they were cocky," she said. "Black Frost thought that Monarch City would crumble against our might, but they didn't."

"What are you talking about? They did surrender, according to plan. Codd showed up with Dyphestive, of all people, and ruined the plan. Your friend Grey Cloak didn't make matters any easier. They killed our father and my dragon." He seethed. "I will get them. I will get both of them."

"Perhaps if we were nicer to them when they were younger, none of this would have happened. They would have stayed and become one of us," she suggested.

"You have a strange perspective, sister. I wish you would gum up." Dirklen scooted back into a corner and turned his back to her. The day had been bad enough, and he didn't want to finish it with her babbling. Magnolia wasn't stupid, and he knew that she only spoke to annoy him. Regardless, it still got under his skin every time.

"Brother," she said.

He cringed.

"Does the scar that Black Frost gave you still burn? I only ask because mine does. It wakes me in my sleep. It will go away, won't it?"

He touched the gash on his cheek. It still burned deep, a constant reminder of his failure that would live with him the rest of his days. "Get used to it."

"I won't ever get used to it, I think. It makes me angry."

"It makes me angry too. It's a nuisance, much like your voice."

"Don't be so nasty to me, dear brother. I'm all that you have. And you never had any other friends to begin with anyway."

He looked over his shoulder. Magnolia had made herself

comfortable on her bed of straw and closed her eyes. Her words rang true, and they stung. The truth was that he didn't have any friends aside from her and their mother and father. He'd never felt close to any of them either. He remembered years ago, seeing Grey Cloak and Dyphestive laughing with others. He hated them for it. He didn't know why, but he did.

"Magnolia," he said quietly.

"Yes?"

"I wish I had a pillow."

"Why is that, brother?"

"So I could smother you with it."

Magnolia let out a goofy giggle. "I'd like to see you try it."

34

Talon traveled unmolested toward Great River many long days on end. They stuck to the back trails, following Tatiana's lead. Grey Cloak used Streak to spy any trouble from the sky.

It was a solemn journey through beautiful countryside filled with every flower and tree imaginable. Groves of incredible oaks stood over five hundred feet high. The deep green and golden leaves were so large that a man could make a blanket out of them.

Being a full elf, Grey Cloak should have appreciated the trip more, but his heart was unsettled. He'd left Anya out in the cold. She didn't have anyone left, and he'd all but abandoned her. He'd been riding in the rear, hood-covered head down, isolated from the others.

Dyphestive rode alongside him. He didn't say anything at first, as he was busy crushing nuts that had fallen from the trees. "These nuts are good. Not very filling but good. Have some?"

"I'll pass, but thanks."

"We haven't talked much, but I wanted to say I'm glad that you wanted to stay with Talon. I wished Anya would have remained, but well, I wanted you to know that I think you did the right thing."

"If I did the right thing, it doesn't feel like it. I spent a lot of time training with her and the others. She'd been with them her entire life." He lowered his head again. "Now, she doesn't have anybody."

"She could have come with us."

"No, she wouldn't stay away from Cinder so long. It must have been hard enough to depart from him to begin with. All on account of me. I feel guilty."

Dyphestive dusted the crumbs off his hands and said, "I feel guilty too."

"Why?"

He shrugged. "We are different, being naturals, and Anya was one of us. I can't explain it, but I feel different from the others somehow."

Eyeing the others, Grey Cloak asked, "Then why are we following them?"

"I don't think that we are following her. We are following you."

"Me?"

"You are the one that agreed to go to the Wizard Watch. If you hadn't, I'm pretty sure everyone else would have followed you elsewhere. Well, besides Tatiana and her henchman."

"Do you really think that?"

"I do."

"Huh." He sat up in his saddle. "I'm pretty sure Zora is mad at me. She hasn't spoken to me since Anya left."

"You haven't spoken to her either. But neither have I. If I do, Leena gets mad. At least, I think she is mad." He lifted his shoulders and gave a perplexed look. "I can't tell because she always looks mad."

"What sort of relationship have you gotten yourself into?"

"I don't know what to call it. How can I call it anything when she doesn't even talk?"

Grey Cloak laughed.

At that very moment, Leena turned and glared at both of them. Dyphestive noticeably shrank in his saddle, like he was trying to dodge her stare.

Grey Cloak couldn't help but chuckle. "Ha-ha, I'm pretty sure she sees you. She's like the little hound that runs the bigger pack. Why are you scared of her? She can't hurt you."

"I don't know. But she does. What do I do?"

"Apparently, whatever she tells you to." He laughed again.

"She doesn't tell me anything, but I'm still doing it." Dyphestive caught her stare. "I'd better get back up there. We'll talk later, when she sleeps. Though I don't even know if she sleeps. I wake up every day with her staring into my eyes." He trotted away.

Zora drifted back from the pack. "It's good to see a smile on your face. I never took you for the kind that sulks. Have you finally gotten over the loss of your woman?"

"My woman? Come now, Zora, you know I only have eyes for you."

"Is that so? Is that why you haven't been speaking to me for the duration of this trip?"

"No," he said as a yellow-and-black butterfly passed by his face. "I apologize for that, but I had the feeling you were mad at me."

"You aren't a complete fool. I *was* mad at you, but I'm over it. I have been for the last few days." Zora's green eyes searched his. "Anya is very beautiful. You care deeply for her. I can tell."

"We have a bond that I'm not going to deny, but it's not romantic in any sort of way. Like you, we've been through a lot together, and now she's alone." He leaned back and stretched. "What can I say? I feel guilty. Wouldn't you?"

"Over her, no. She can take care of herself."

He couldn't hide his surprise and said, "She's lost everything."

"Including her humility, if she ever had any to begin with. She's very arrogant."

"Zora, her entire family and everyone she has ever known was killed by Black Frost. Your horseshoe would be bent too."

She shook her head. "First, I've never known my parents. Second, neither have you. Third, neither one of us acts as awful as she did."

Grey Cloak's shoulders sank. "She might be rigid, but once you get to know her, she really isn't that bad."

"Is that right?" Zora's cheeks turned red, and her expression darkened. "Look at you, making excuses and defending her. Shame on you, Grey Cloak. Where was she when we were fighting for our lives in Monarch City? Where was she when our necks were in nooses? Did she say that she was there? Funny, I didn't see her, but do you know who I did see? I saw Tatiana. She risked her life to save all of us. And there you sit, tall in your saddle, with all of the answers, without so much as thanking her, but instead accusing her of misleading us."

"You didn't really come back here to make up with me, did you?"

"No, I came to talk sense into you."

"Well, you're doing a fine job of it!"

"Good!"

"Good!" She slapped her reins and rode away.

Grey Cloak bobbed in his saddle as he trailed behind the others. He couldn't help but smile and say, "I suppose that could have gone worse."

35

Great River ran from the peaks of the east to the forests of Gapoli in the south, feeding the woodland and farms of the elvish lands along the way. As the gray clouds gathered and a steady rain came down, Talon traveled down grassy slopes toward Great River with Tatiana still leading the way.

"We'll cross the bridge at Doverpoint," she said as she pulled her robes tight around her to protect against the rain, "and travel north to the Wizard Watch, another two days' journey."

Lighting flashed, and thunder began to roll.

"Are there towns on the other side of the villages?" Crane asked as he held his pudgy hand out and caught the rain. "It hasn't rained for the entire journey, and I've become accustomed to staying dry."

"There are," she said. "I'm surprised that you didn't know that."

"I've never traveled to the other side of Great River. I heard it is an untamed land."

"It's not without its savages." Tatiana sat up and stared down into the valley. "That's odd. There are garrisons of elves at the bridge. "I'll ride down and see what is happening."

"I'll go with you," Grey Cloak offered.

"There is no need—"

"I insist. After all, we are both elves. I'm sure they'll take a shine to us." He smirked. "Well, me, maybe."

"You and your humor. Come, then." Tatiana trotted down to the riverbank.

They didn't make it within one hundred feet of the bridge before they were surrounded by the garrison.

Grey Cloak had seen plenty of elves in his lifetime but never such a large cluster at once. Most of them were tall and lean, with silky hair hanging down past their necks. They were well dressed and refined looking in soft leather armor that was dyed shades of brown, green, red, and orange that blended into the woodland. They carried bows and feathered arrows, and a longsword and two daggers decorated every hip. He nodded at one of the women. She didn't bat a lash.

An elven soldier with silvery-white hair and a white

scar splitting his chin approached Tatiana. "I am Captain Edyrn Silvius. State your name and business."

"I'm Tatiana, and this is Grey Cloak." Tatiana raised an eyebrow. "I have business in West Arrowwood and seek passage across the Doverpoint bridge."

"That won't be possible, Tatiana," the captain said. He unrolled a scroll and handed it to her. "This is from the elven Monarch herself. The quill point is fine, but I'd be happy to summarize it. Currently, the feud on both sides of the river has enhanced." He pointed at his garrison of soldiers and the soldiers on the other side of the bridge. "The West River elves guard our side of the bridges, and the East River elves guard theirs."

Tatiana scanned the scroll. "This is not good. The Monarch Queen has declared the West River elves enemies of the Monarchy. She has stopped all travel and commerce on both sides of the river." She dropped her gaze to Captain Edyrn Silvius and returned the scroll. "This is more than a feud. It's a declaration of war."

"Call it what you will. They're the Monarch Queen's orders just the same. I'm glad to stand by them. The West River elves now keep unseemly company with orcs, gnolls, and other sorts that have trekked over the Green Hills to taint our valleys." He looked like he was about to spit. "Of course, all of this could be avoided if the West River elves will turn over a single traitor."

"All of this over one man? Who?" she asked.

The captain handed her a rolled-up leather parchment. "We are seeking out this elf. Have you come across him in your travels?"

"There are many elves," she said as she unrolled the scroll. "He's distinguished. If I'd seen him, I would remember."

She handed it back, and the captain gave it to Grey Cloak.

"What about you?" he asked.

Grey Cloak's heart skipped. There was no mistaking the hard eyes and strong angular features of Bowbreaker. "I have to say, I'm new to Arrowwood, and I haven't encountered many elves either, aside from today. But this one, I'd remember if I had seen him. I'm curious—how can one elf stir up so much trouble?"

"He threatens the Monarchy. And he is a West River elf, and they harbor him." The captain took the scroll from Grey Cloak and rolled it up. "He is a very bad man."

"If this Bowbreaker is being harbored by the West River elves, why, pray tell, are you looking for him on this side?" Tatiana asked.

"Because there are many conspirators that serve Bowbreaker's brood. That's why I ask everyone that comes and goes. His spies make use of these bridges. All it takes is the bat of an eye when I show them that picture, or perhaps their ears perk up when I mention his name." He swung his gaze up to Grey Cloak. "Just like yours did. Soldiers, seize them!"

36

Grey Cloak and Tatiana were hauled off to a small jail set up not far from the Doverpoint bridge. The jail was a simple structure, hastily made from wooden logs and rusting iron doors. The roof wasn't well thatched, and rain dripped inside steadily, making the dirt floor pure mud.

"Another fine situation you have gotten us into," Grey Cloak said.

"Me? You were the one with the big eyes at the mentioning of Bowbreaker. Talk about a guilty countenance. A blind man could have seen it." She kept her robes lifted above her boots and tried to avoid the rain in the corner of the room. Drops of water trickled off her shoulder. "From here on out, let me do the talking."

"If you wish." Grey Cloak curled up in his cloak.

Despite the sloppy and damp conditions, he was quite comfortable inside the gray garment. "I'll keep my lips sealed. Not a word from me. After all, you are the smart one."

She sighed and said, "You're never going to like me, are you?"

"Let me say that I don't care much for how your kind operates. Anya was onto something when she called you out. I could see it in your eyes. It stuck with me."

"Anya sees what she wants."

"And you don't?"

A long silence followed.

When Grey Cloak had first met Talon back in Raven Cliff, he was fascinated by Tatiana. She was poised, beautiful, and very personal. But since she'd been charged with handling the dragon charms, she'd been nothing short of prickly. Even her beauty couldn't overcome the edge that she carried. Unlike Dalsay, it wasn't well suited for her.

"You aren't the only one that lost much," she said sadly. "I lost Dalsay, my brothers, not to mention Adanadel and Browning. We were close. All of us. Believe me when I say that it hurts when I think about them. You make me out to be a frosty witch. I am not. Forgive me for trying to do the right thing the best way I know how."

Grey Cloak shifted uncomfortably. He found her irritating but felt sorry for her at the same time. *Maybe she does have a heart.* "Thanks," he muttered.

"What was that?"

"I said thanks."

"For what?"

"Saving me and the rest of us, back at Monarch Castle." He caught her eye. "You saved my neck from the noose, and I'm grateful."

"Thank you."

"I know you are trying, Tatiana, but what I don't know is what we are doing. I'm sorry to bring it up, but you've been gathering dragon charms for how long? Years? A decade? And where are they?"

Shamefaced, she said, "I don't know. If I did, I'd tell you. And I'm not without my doubts either, but my faith in the Wizard Watch is all that I have."

"Perhaps it's time that you put your faith in something else."

"Like what?"

"Your friends."

"If I didn't have faith in you, do you think that I'd risk my life to save you?"

"Good point." He eyed the ceiling, which was still dripping water. "I think we've hashed this out enough. Do you want to get out of here?"

"Yes, but we can't blast out and bring an elven garrison down on us. This is a delicate situation," she said as she watched the water drain from her robes. "Apparently, the situation with Bowbreaker is direr than I realized."

"I know little about him."

"It is said that he is the one destined to slay the evil Monarch Queen. I find it difficult to believe that Esmeralda is evil."

"Perhaps he's being framed."

"Regardless, they will want to peel our skulls open to find out everything we know about him. If we aren't convincing, they'll accuse us of being spies. If that is the case, they'll kill us."

"We shouldn't be punished for knowing him. Perhaps I need to do the talking. I can be very persuasive if you allow me."

"We've both denied knowing him. We have to convince them this is all a misunderstanding. Can you do that?"

Heavier rains began to brew outside, and the muddy floor was overrun with dripping water. He smirked. "Sit back and watch me. I only hope that the others don't try anything silly."

"WE NEED TO GET THEM," Dyphestive said. Talon remained hidden in a grove overlooking the Doverpoint bridge. The rain poured down as they eyed the small jail, which was surrounded by half a dozen elven soldiers. "The sooner the better."

"We can't storm down there and bully them. There are

at least a thousand elves in these hills," Crane said. "You might not see them, but they are there. It's their lands. They are everywhere. We need to wait it out and see what they want. Perhaps I can find out."

Dyphestive rubbed his jaw. He wasn't sure who was in charge since Grey Cloak and Tatiana were both gone. Perhaps he was, and everyone appeared to be looking to him. The last thing he wanted, however, was for anyone else to get captured. "Why would they arrest them?"

"That's what we need to find out," Crane said.

"I know that," he said.

Zora pecked him on the shoulder. "I'll use the scarf and go."

Dyphestive wiped the water from his brow and looked down at her. She appeared very small to him. In his heart, he didn't want to risk her getting caught either. He wasn't used to placing others in danger. He put his hands on her shoulders and said, "Do it, but be careful."

"Don't worry. This will be easy. I'll be back before the next raindrop hits your nose." She covered the bottom of her face with the black scarf and disappeared.

Dyphestive wiped a raindrop from his nose.

37

Captain Edyrn Silvius held a disgusting-looking creature in front of Grey Cloak's eyes and said, "This is a river leech, a creature of unique traits. Notice that its slimy, gelatinous body is lean, not full of blood as of yet. But when it eats, believe me, it will drain quarts of blood from your body and swell up bigger than your head."

Grey Cloak's lips twisted, and he pulled his head back. He was secured to a chair with his hands tied behind his back and his ankles tied to the chair legs. And elven soldier stood behind him with his strong hands holding down his shoulders. "Well, my head's pretty big, so that would be something."

"Oh, humor. You will need that to get you through the pain that you are about to experience," the captain said.

"That's good to know, but don't you think this is a bit

much? After all, you are accusing us of knowing one elf out of, I don't know, hundreds of thousands."

"Yes, well, there is only one way to be sure if you both won't come clean."

"This is outrageous!" Tatiana was beside Grey Cloak, tied up in the same fashion. "I am a citizen of Arrowwood. You can't torture me."

Captain Edyrn Silvius had come across as a fair-minded elf when they'd first met, but he'd turned sinister. His eyes were cold, and his voice carried a deadly intent. "I have the authority, per the Monarch Queen, to do whatever is required to learn the truth." He swung the foot-long leech over in front of Tatiana's face. "Of course, if you were to admit the truth, we could move away from the uncivilized method of torture."

"You are making a grave mistake, Captain. I'm no ordinary citizen passing through. There will be severe repercussions when my family finds out about this," she said.

"Ah." The captain's face brightened. "So you have close ties to the Monarch Queen. Please tell me, who are they?"

"No, I'll let you hang yourself."

"Hmph." The captain turned his attention back to Grey Cloak. "Do you have any elven family ties that you would like to boast?"

"No." He tilted his head toward Tatiana. "Only her. And between you and me, she's rather difficult," he whispered.

"And if you think she's bad, wait until you meet the rest of her family."

The captain chuckled as large drops of rain splashed on his silvery hair. "Given my age and station, I don't think I have much to lose. Also, I'm one of the Monarch Queen's favorite cousins. Ah-ha. Surprise, surprise." He lowered the leech over Grey Cloak's thigh. "Now tell me what you know about Bowbreaker."

In truth, Grey Cloak couldn't have cared less about Bowbreaker. The big elf was solemn and had the personality of a goat. He wasn't fond of Zora's noticeable attraction to him either. He cleared his throat and said, "Do you think that you could torture Tatiana first? After all, her thighs are bigger than mine."

"They are not!" Tatiana said.

Grey Cloak could have sworn that he heard someone else chuckle, but he couldn't say for sure, as it was quickly drowned out by the rain.

However, the captain eyed the room suspiciously. He let out a sigh and said, "If you aren't going to cooperate, then you give me little choice, but I'll offer you one last chance. What do you know about Bowbreaker?"

"Oh yes, now I remember. He is that elf that breaks bows, isn't he?" He glanced at Tatiana. "Remember. I had a bow, and he took it and broke it over his knee. Or wait, was it over his head?"

"Actually, he broke *my* bow on his head," Tatiana said,

playing along. "And he broke your bow on your head." She let out a bizarre and unbecoming laugh. "Ahahahaha!"

Grey Cloak and the captain gave her appalled looks.

"What?" she asked. "You don't like my laughing?"

"I'm not sure what that was, but it wasn't laughing or cackling or cajoling," Grey Cloak quipped. He leaned toward the captain, looked up, and said, "We're only distant, distant, distant cousins."

"I'd hope. Enough, however. I've extended to you ample opportunities to come clean, and you've mocked them. I don't like that." He dropped the leech onto Grey Cloak's trousers. "You're going to regret not being more cooperative."

The leech latched on, and Grey Cloak dropped his head for a closer look. The fabric of his pants crinkled. He quickly looked up. "It's going to take forever to press that back out. Well done, Captain Edyrn Silvius. Well done indeed!"

The captain smirked.

Grey Cloak's face puckered as the leech latched through his pants and onto his leg. "Gah!" He stared wide-eyed at his leg. The leech began bulging, and he could feel the blood flowing out of his thigh.

"Now, if you like, Grey Cloak, you can tell me what you know about Bowbreaker, or I can let the leech—or rather, leeches—drain all the blood from your body."

Excruciating pain lanced through his body from the top

of his head to his toes. He could feel his heart beating behind his eyeballs. The pain was killing him. He clenched his jaw. *Hang on! Don't give in! You're stronger than him! It's only a leech, after all! And how much blood do I really need anyway?*

By the time he looked back down, the leech had more than doubled in size. *Zooks, I have a lot of blood.*

He glanced at Tatiana. There was no mistaking her horrified expression. She looked as if he was about to die.

"Stop this, Captain! Stop this!" she said.

"Oh, it is quite too late for that. Of course, if you would shed more light on Bowbreaker, then I would be more than happy to help you."

Grey Cloak's voice came out as a pant. "We don't know anything."

Captain Edyrn Silvius whispered in his ear, "We'll know the very truth of the matter soon enough."

38

The leech grew bigger, and Grey Cloak's stomach turned inside out. The bulging leech was one of the most disgusting things that he'd ever seen, and it was attached to his leg. He became light-headed, and his neck rolled to the side. "Will you stop this?"

"Soon, the blood loss will be so great that you will tell me whatever I want," Captain Silvius said. "It is one of the glorious effects of this rudimentary torture."

"Come closer," Grey Cloak said in a raspy voice. "I want to tell you something."

"Of course." The captain bent over and offered his ear. "What is it that you want to say?"

"I-I…"

"Yes?"

"I really don't like you."

Captain Silvius frowned and rose back up. "This one is very stubborn." He lifted Grey Cloak's chin. "You should have spilled the information by now."

"Let him go!" Tatiana said. "Can't you see he doesn't know anything?" The leech had swollen as thick as an elf's forearm. "You're going to kill him!"

As his blood drained, Grey Cloak's head sank toward his chest. It felt like it was made of sand, and he couldn't lift it.

"Tell me about Bowbreaker, Grey Cloak. I know that you want to tell me. I've been doing this a long time, and I know that you know something. Tell me," the captain urged.

The pain in Grey Cloak's body subsided, and it was replaced by a euphoric feeling. He drooled and smiled. "Oh yes, my friend Bowbreaker." He shook his head. "He doesn't smile." He gave a big frown. "Looks like this all the time. Sort of like you, Captain Leechbottom."

"Now we are getting somewhere, aren't we?" The captain eyeballed Tatiana. "It appears that someone was lying. Well, the truth always comes out, doesn't it?"

With his vision fading, Grey Cloak noticed an indentation the size of a foot in the mud beside the captain. He giggled. "I know someone that likes Bowbreaker."

Pffft! A white mist sprayed under Captain Silvius's nose. His nostrils widened as he inhaled deeply. He tried to jump away from the cloud, but his legs turned into noodles, and he splashed face-first onto the muddy floor.

Grey Cloak was all smiles when Zora appeared. She moved in a blur and struck the elf soldier behind him.

A bright flash and a smell of burning rope followed. Two more elven soldiers were knocked out at his feet.

"Zora?" He practically sang when he said it. "Someone is looking for your boyfriend."

"Bloody horseshoes, he's a mess," Zora said as she stared at the leech. "Uck! It's disgusting. How do we get this thing off of him?"

"I'm not sure," Tatiana said, her brow furrowed.

Zora tried to pry the leech off with her fingers. "Ew, it's so slimy. My hands won't stick to it."

"Don't touch my friend," Grey Cloak said, slurring his speech. "He's not an it. He has a name. Do you want to know what it is?"

"Why not?" Zora said.

"It's Bowbreaker. Ahahahahah!"

Zora rolled her eyes and pulled a dagger. "I'll skin it off."

"No, no, don't kill Bowbreaker," Grey Cloak pleaded. "He's my friend." He sobbed. "A good friend. Slimy but good. Hello, Zora. Are you doing something different with your hair? It looks slimy too. Ouch!"

"This might hurt, but it has to come off. And keep it down."

"Let me try something," Tatiana said. "You cut him loose." Her fingertips glowed white, and she touched the leech.

Popsplurp! The bloody leech exploded all over them.

Grey Cloak's chin quivered. "You killed my friend. You killed my friend Bowbreaker."

Zora wiped the bloody grit from her face and cut him free. "We'll get you another one."

"But I liked that one." He looked at his bloody thigh. "Bye-bye, Bowbreaker."

"Goodness, how much blood did he lose?" Zora asked.

Tatiana gathered their belongings from crude hooks on the wall and held the Star of Light in her palm. "Good, it's all here. It will take some time to get him back to normal. In the meantime, we need to get out of here. How are the others?"

"Waiting for me," Zora said. She helped Grey Cloak to his feet. "Why do they want Bowbreaker?"

"It appears that the Monarch Queen has a bounty on his head." Tatiana bent to one knee and bound the captain. "Help me drag them to the cell."

Zora grabbed the captain's feet, and Tatiana picked him up by the arms. They shuffled toward the cell.

"Why does the Monarch Queen want Bowbreaker?" Zora asked.

"Because he's destined to killed her."

Zora dropped the captain. "Oh."

As they hauled the other two soldiers away, Grey Cloak sat in his chair, neck wobbling, and said, "You ladies are doing a fine, fine job. It's good to see you two working together."

"Can you walk?" Zora asked him.

"Can I walk? Pfft! Of course I can. Watch this." Grey Cloak stood, took a bow, and fell down. He kicked his feet and rolled over to his side. With mud all over his hands, he said, "Zooks, who moved the floor on me?"

Zora and Tatiana exchanged befuddled looks.

"What are we going to do? We can't sneak him out of here like this," Zora said.

Tatiana took a peek out of the jail's front door, which was little more than a flap. It was still pouring with rain. She turned and said, "I have an idea, but we have to act quickly."

39

Zora wrapped the Scarf of Shadows around Grey Cloak's neck and said, "We are going to walk you out of here, but you have to stand. We'll help you."

Grey Cloak gave her a lazy-eyed look, toyed with the scarf, and said, "This doesn't look good on me. Not my style."

"Will you please work with me?"

He made a sour face and said, "I'll try."

Tatiana began putting on the captain's leather armor.

"Oh, look at that. She's already turned traitor. I knew it."

Tatiana rolled her eyes and shook her head. "No one is turning traitor. It's a disguise, you fool."

"Fool? I'm no fool. No fool at all. You are a fool."

"Lords of the Air, what did that leech do to him?" Zora

asked as she hauled him to his feet and propped him against the wall.

"Apparently, it damaged his gray matter. We can only hope it isn't permanent." Tatiana relieved Zora and held him steady on the wall. "You have to behave, Grey Cloak. We are escaping, but you must cooperate. Follow our lead. Do you understand?"

He nodded, touched her lips, and played with them. "You have soft lips." He poked them. "I saw an orc with lips like yours. She was a waitress at the Tavern Dwellers Inn. Called Marmie."

Tatiana covered his mouth while Zora slipped on another leather tunic. "I don't have puffy orc lips."

His words muffled by her hand, he said, "Yes, you do."

Tatiana shot a look at Zora and said, "I'm doing this." She covered his nose with the scarf, and he disappeared.

"Where did I go? Help me!" he cried. "I can't see me!"

Tatiana pinched his arm tight. "Be still!"

"But I can't see myself. Oh no! I'm a ghost like Dalsay, roaming the spirit world while still consorting with elven witches."

"I'm not a witch!" Tatiana said.

"Funny, I can feel myself, but I can't see myself. Hmm... I wonder what will happen if I relieve myself. I have to pee."

"Zora, get over here!" Tatiana said as she wrestled to hang on to Grey Cloak. "Grab an arm. We need to go."

Managing to latch onto Grey Cloak's arm, Zora said, "Close your eyes and let us guide you. Remember, you have the Scarf of Shadows on. No one is supposed to see you."

"Ah yes, the Scarf of Shadows. I like it. Where is it?" he said.

"I'm ready," Zora said.

Tatiana filled her hand with the Star of Light. "I'm going to summon my power that will conceal our identities. With the help of the armor and the weather, we should fool the elven soldiers. Let's go."

Grey Cloak stumbled between them with their arms locked around his elbows. They stepped right out of the jail and into the pouring rain.

"My, this is dreary. Am I wet if I can't see myself dripping?"

"Shh!" Zora said.

She took the lead, moving away from the Doverpoint bridge and toward the rise that looked over the river. Grey Cloak half dragged his feet and splashed through muddy puddles. She couldn't see him, but she could see the trail he was making. "Will you stop that?"

"No, because you can't see me."

A trio of elven soldiers was posted along the road that led to the bridge. They cut them off, and one asked, "Where are you headed on a night like this? And why are you walking like that?"

Zora's heart thumped rapidly. She squeezed Grey

Cloak's arm, thinking, *Don't you say a word. Please don't say a word.*

"Captain Silvius is not pleased with us. We are to gather wood for the fires. In this!" Tatiana said in a harsh imitation of a manly voice. "Don't ever drop an eyelid on his watch," she added.

"Ah," one of the elves said. "He's as hard as a black walnut. Good luck finding timber that will light in this weather."

The trio of soldiers nodded and moved down the slope toward the road.

"That was close," Zora muttered.

"You have big behinds!" Grey Cloak shouted at the soldiers. "Like ogres!"

Zora and Tatiana hurried up the hill, glancing over their shoulders, but the hard rain must have drowned out Grey Cloak's voice, because elven soldiers marched down the hill without so much as a backward glance.

"You fool, you're going to get us caught," Tatiana said. "From here on out, stifle it!"

"I'm a ghost. Therefore, I can do and *say* whatever I want," he replied. "Ogre bottom."

They continued up the hill, leaving the road to the bridge far behind. They ventured straight to the grove, where Grunt and Razor confronted them.

"It's us," Zora said as she pulled down the scarf from Grey Cloak's face.

"Ah, I'm alive again," he said.

They released him, and he collapsed on the ground. Grunt tilted his head and grunted.

"What's the matter with him?" Razor asked.

"A river leech sucked half of his gray matter out."

Razor's lip curled. "Ew... I've seen that happen before."

Dyphestive rushed over, dropped to his knees, and asked, "What's wrong?"

"He's fine," Zora answered. "Pick him up, and let's go."

Once again, Talon was united.

"Everyone, listen," Tatiana said. "We have to cross that bridge one way or the other before every West River elf in Arrowwood starts hunting us down. I can conceal myself and Grey Cloak in the rain, to some degree, but we have to take our chances now. They are only looking for the two of us." She looked at Crane. "You'll have to use that silver tongue to talk us across. It's the only way."

Crane nodded. "Everyone, mount up. Tatiana, you and Grey Cloak hop in."

Crane took the lead, with Tatiana and Grey Cloak hunkered down in the back of the wagon, Zora rode beside them, and the others rode behind.

"I want to ride a horse," Grey Cloak said.

There was a stir down at the Doverpoint bridge. The garrison of elves had clustered together, and most of them were carrying torches. The moment they spotted the wagon coming, the elves stopped and pointed, and the hard rains let up. Captain Silvius stood among them, mouthing orders.

Zora exchanged concerned looks with Tatiana and said, "We fooled them once. I don't think we'll fool them twice."

The West River elves were coming.

40

Crane lifted his carriage whip and said, "I hope enough time has passed."

Grey Cloak reached for it. "Let me do it. I want to do it!"

Tatiana pulled him down into the wagon and covered his nose with the scarf. "Be still!" She eyed Crane. "Do what you will."

Crane flicked the carriage lash, and it immediately caught fire. "Ho-ho!" His eyes burned like the flames of a candle as he cracked Vixen on the back. "Onward, Vixen! Onward!"

The wagon lurched forward and quickly gained speed. Grey Cloak slid to the back and slammed into the gate. He shook his head, grabbed the side, and hung on.

The wheels were spinning flames, and Vixen's hooves were on fire. The wagon roared down the hill.

Behind the wagon, the rest of Talon rode hard. The horses labored to keep up. Arrows zinged through the air and whistled by their heads.

Tatiana rose in her seat and lifted the Star of Light. The gem emanated white light through cracks of her curled fingers. A shield of energy spread out over the back of the wagon, covering the horse and riders.

With the wind tearing at his face, Grey Cloak crawled toward the front. His strength was returning, and he sat up on his knees behind the bench.

A garrison of elven soldiers barricaded the bridge with large spiked beams that were shaped like jacks. The elves were clustered around blockages, some with spears in hand and others firing arrows.

"Can you make it through that?" Grey Cloak asked.

Crane winked and said, "We'll know in a moment."

Grey Cloak's head began to clear. He took one last glance behind his shoulder before they crashed to their doom. The wagon left twin trails of flames behind it. Talon rode between the trails, hunkered down over their horses.

Arrows ricocheted off Tatiana's shield. Grunt thundered down the path in the back. A dozen elves sped right behind him, shooting arrows at his back.

"Hold on!" Crane said.

Grey Cloak whipped his head around in time to see the nightmare horse, Vixen, plow full speed into the elven ranks and barricades. The big-eyed elves hopped out of the way like scared rabbits, fear filling their eyes, as the Wheels of Fire careened through the first blockade. The large timbers popped and cracked.

"Yah, Vixen! Yah!" Crane hollered.

The blockades and troops were three rows deep. Vixen tore through every last one, setting everything on fire and sending flaming elves off the bridge and into the river.

Grey Cloak looked backward and frontward, not believing his eyes. Not only had the wagon cleared the blockades, but Talon had, too, including Grunt, who had a back full of arrows. They were riding hard right behind them.

"Ah-ha!" Grey Cloak exclaimed. "You did it, Crane!"

"It's not over yet!" Crane set his eyes on the road ahead. The East River elves had gathered at the far end of the bridge and formed a tight group. "Should I slow?"

"No. Keep rolling!"

"Roll, Vixen! Roll!" Crane shouted.

The Wheels of Fire thundered over the wooden planks of the bridge, setting the structure aflame.

The West River elves were closing in. At the last moment, they split left and right and passed right by the wagon. In seconds, a full garrison of West River elves cut off the East River elves' pursuit. The coast was clear to the other side of the bridge.

Vixen raced on. The wheels clattered over the wood,

and the flames started to die down. At the end of the bridge, Vixen slowed.

"What's wrong?" Grey Cloak asked.

"That's a long bridge. She's whipped," Crane said as the wagon rolled to a stop.

The last flames on the horse hooves and wagon wheels went out. A lathered-up Vixen snorted and labored for breath. In the blink of an eye, Talon, wagon and all, was surrounded by the East River elves five rows deep.

The elves, dressed in leather tunics, stood in the rain, staring at the company with hardened eyes. Their hands were filled with spears and bows and arrows. Every one of them was too close to miss.

Grey Cloak pushed himself up to standing and said, "Excuse me, brethren, but could someone tell us how to get to Breckenridge Dales? We are horribly off course and ..." His head started to swim, the rainy skies spiraled, and the world he knew turned black.

41

Fresh morning air tickled Grey Cloak's nose, and the sun shone through his eyelids. His head lay on a warm pillow of sorts that was comfortable if not odd. He cracked an eye open and found himself looking at Zora, who had a distant expression on her face.

She dropped her stare, and he closed his eye. He was comfortable in her warm lap and didn't have any desire to leave. *No sense in spoiling a good thing. Especially given that the last time we spoke, she was mad at me.*

Zora gently brushed his hair to the side and caressed his face from his forehead to his chin.

This is nice. I knew she liked me.

Her hand cradled his chin and cheeks.

Ah, very nice.

She started to apply more pressure.

Uh, what is she doing? Easy, Zora. My elven features are delicate, after all.

The way her fingernails bit into his skin felt as if a crab had ahold of him.

I'm starting to think that she might not be the best mate after all.

Zora shook his face and said, "I know that you are awake. I saw you looking. Do you mind? My legs are numb from sitting so long."

He sat up and bumped his head into her chin.

"Ow," she said in an irritated manner.

"Sorry."

"It's fine. I'm used to you being a pain."

Grey Cloak got his first look at his surroundings. Crane drove the wagon, Tatiana sitting beside him. Neither one of them looked back at him. To his right and left were East River elven soldiers in forest-colored tunics, marching on foot. Behind them were the other members of Talon on horseback. Grunt still had arrows sticking out of his back.

When Grey Cloak caught Dyphestive's eye, his solemn expression brightened, but it was quickly extinguished when Leena gave him a hard look. He mouthed, "Later," to Grey Cloak.

"What is happening?" Grey Cloak asked.

"Keep your voice down," Zora warned quietly. "I'll explain shortly. How are you feeling?"

"Not awful," he said, even though his head was swimming a little. "How long have I been asleep?"

"Two days."

"Two—"

Zora clamped her hand over his mouth. "I said keep it down. I don't need you to call the river elves a bunch of orc bottoms like you've called everyone else."

"Orc bottoms? When did I say that?"

"In Captain Silvius's jail."

He raised an eyebrow. "I don't remember that."

"What do you remember?"

"I remember the jail and the river leech," he said as he glanced at his thigh, which had a bandage around it. "Gah! What happened?"

"The leech was attached to it." She shook her head. "I need to take a look. There were tiny teeth in your leg that I had to pick out."

"Tiny teeth?" He watched in horror as Zora unwrapped the bandage. That was when he noticed that half of his trouser leg had been cut off. "I need new pants."

"That's not all that you need," she said.

His thigh had a large purple bruise on it and a raised white ring, like teeth marks. "That's awful."

"It was worse when I wrapped it. According to the East River elves, you could have lost your leg if it hadn't been treated."

"I don't remember it feeling that bad, except at first."

"Yes, I don't think you were feeling anything." She

wrapped the leg back up. "Can you bend it?"

Gritting his teeth, he drew his leg toward his chest and grunted. "It's stiff, but I'm sure I can walk." He glanced about. They were surrounded by miles of elven countryside that was the envy of the world. "Not that I need to. Where are we going?"

"North, to the Wizard Watch." Zora eyeballed the back of Tatiana's braided hair. "We were fortunate that Tatiana's cousins were among the East River elves when we crossed. They vouched for her, and she vouched for us. Now, they escort us to the tower, however far that might be."

For the first time, Tatiana turned her head and acknowledged Grey Cloak. "I'm glad to see you awake."

"I bet you are," he said. "Are you taking us to the witch tower where you were born?"

Zora giggled. "You're definitely feeling better. Good."

"I really am impressed with the countryside," Crane commented. His eyes were puffy, and his gaze darted about. "So many different trees and birds. It's another part of the world, so unlike the rest. Maybe we don't ever need to go back across the river. I can build a camp and live out the rest of my days here."

"The streams are rich in fish. A single day's outing will feed you for days," Tatiana said. "I spent many years living on the banks in my youth. I miss it."

Crane scooted closer to her until their hips touched. "Perhaps we can make a new life together."

Tatiana jumped out of the wagon and said, "I don't think so. I'm committed to a ghost."

"How long can that last?" Crane asked with a sparkle in his eye as he watched her walking away. "My, she is dazzling, isn't she?"

"I've seen more dazzling," Grey Cloak said with his eyes on Zora.

She shoved his head back. "Stop doing that."

"Do I need to thank you for saving me?"

"Yes," she said with a playful smile on her lips while her fingers toyed with her scarf. "But a simple thank you will do. After all, you saved me too."

"Thank you, Zora." He took her hand and squeezed it.

"It was nothing."

She didn't release his hand, and they both sat back and relaxed.

Tatiana had made her way through the elven ranks and caught up with a soldier in the front. He stood tall and wore a grim expression, and his shock of black hair was short. They engaged in a heated conversation before Tatiana wandered back. Her brow was furrowed more than usual.

Zora broke away from Grey Cloak, slid over to the other side of the wagon, and asked, "What's wrong?"

"My cousin states that they cannot escort us any farther after today. We are on our own from here," Tatiana said.

"Is that bad?"

Tatiana nodded. "The woodland is wild. It isn't good."

42

Talon made camp that evening in a cherry tree grove at the edge of a forest. Jakoby dropped branches onto the fire. Crane hummed a cheerful tune as he stared into the fire. Razor was busy digging the last two arrows out of Grunt's back.

"Doesn't that hurt?" Zora asked with a sour face.

"These little arrows hurt Grunt?" Razor said in his rugged but charming manner. "Hardly. His hide is thicker than the Rogues of Rodden. If anything, these arrows help him with his itchy spots." He pulled an arrow out and scratched Grunt's back with it.

Grunt stamped his hoof on the ground and bent a horn over his shoulder.

"See? He likes it," Razor said with a grin.

"I can see that." Zora moved away to where Grey Cloak was waiting by the fire.

He patted a spot on the ground for her. "Care to sit?" he asked, offering a warm smile. He felt closer to her than he ever had, and he liked it. "I won't bite."

"No, your bark is worse than your bite." She sat and braced her back against a log that Tatiana was sitting on. "Do we have far to go?"

"It depends," Tatiana said.

"Depends on what?" Grey Cloak asked.

"On what we may or may not encounter. These are the wilds, and they are full of many dangerous surprises."

He straightened his back and said, "I'm sorry, but I was under the impression that you were born here and that you might have traveled this direction many times before."

"No," Tatiana said as she tightened the cloak around her shoulders.

"Tatiana, that doesn't make any sense. You have been to this Wizard Watch before, haven't you?"

"Yes, of course I have," she said as she stared deeply into the fire.

Many in the company exchanged confused looks with one another.

Grey Cloak started to grind his teeth. "You aren't making any sense, Tatiana, and it's getting under my skin. Do explain."

"I can't," Tatiana replied. "What happens in the Wizard Watch stays in the Wizard Watch."

"What are you talking about?" Jakoby's rich voice rose. "This is not Talagon City that you are speaking of. It's a wizard tower."

Not hiding her irritation, she said, "I'm sorry, but I am not allowed to speak about the Watch. I swore an oath. Our journey would be more pleasant if you would trust me."

"Dirty acorns, Tat!" Zora said. "You never tell us anything."

"Was Dalsay any less vague when you dealt with him?" Tatiana fired back.

"We never had our backs to the wall with Dalsay," Zora replied.

Tatiana sighed and lifted her hands. "I'm sorry. But you have to trust me. I'm certain that your questions will be answered when we arrive at the Wizard Watch. In the meantime, rest well. It will be a treacherous journey on the morrow."

Streak dropped out of the sky and landed beside Grey Cloak, causing Zora to jump out of her seat.

Clutching her chest, she said, "Streak, you scared the nails off my toes."

A field mouse the size of a cat hung dead in Streak's flat snout. He set the mouse down by her toes.

Zora gently nudged it away with her boot. "Thank you, but I'm not hungry. You can have it."

"He likes you," Grey Cloak said as he patted Streak's head. "Perhaps more than me. He's never offered me a rodent before."

"You can have it," she said.

He noticed Grunt's big spacey eyes locked on it. "Streak, why don't you take it over to him?"

"Don't bother," Razor said. "Grunt doesn't eat meat. He lives off vegetation." He passed his hands over Grunt's eyes. "I can't say for sure, but I think the big rat scares him."

Grey Cloak picked the field mouse up by the tail and tossed it over the fire at Grunt, who jumped up and dashed into the darkness of the surrounding woodland.

"I'd say you are right."

"Why did you do that for? Now I have to go find him." Razor stuck the arrows into the ground and followed Grunt.

Dyphestive caught his attention with a wave of his hand. He was sitting beside Leena, who was on her knees, eyes closed in meditation. She was perfectly composed, as still as a statue in her silky black robes with gold trim on the sleeves.

"Excuse me," Dyphestive said to Zora, "but it's high time that I caught up with my brother."

She nodded.

They moved away from the campfire, out of earshot, and stood underneath the ebony tapestry of a star-filled sky.

Dyphestive let out a sigh as he glanced back at Leena. "I'm sorry, Grey. I've been meaning to check on you, but Leena, well, she's possessive."

He glanced at her. "She's no bigger than a wart on a frog's bottom."

"But she hits like a mule kicks."

"Do you like her?"

"I don't know." Dyphestive's big paw of a hand rubbed the back of his neck. "I guess. But she's possessive. What do I do?"

"You're asking me? I don't know. Is this what you brought me over here to talk about?"

"No. Well, yes and no. I only wanted to talk and make sure you are well. How is the leg?"

"I'm a tad gimpy but over it for the most part. How are you?"

Dyphestive shrugged. "As healthy as a horse." He eyed the camp. "What do you think about Tatiana and Anya? Do you believe what Anya said? Can we trust Tatiana?"

Grey Cloak smirked. "I'm not sure, but for now, I'll take my chances."

43

ANYA

"Idiots," Anya said under her breath. "Idiots. Idiots. Idiots."

It was the middle of the night, and steady rain was coming down. She was in the middle of crossing Great River about half a league north of the Doverpoint bridge. Using a log she'd found on the riverbank as a raft, she paddled with the stream, hoping to avoid the ever-alert river elves that patrolled the banks.

Great River's current was swift, carrying her quickly down the wide channel back toward the Doverpoint bridge. She paddled her feet as fast as she could, aiming for the dark, sandy banks on the other side. Her dragon armor, though light, was still more than heavy enough to drag her down into the water. If she let go, she would sink to the bottom and certainly die a watery death. She clutched the log and kicked faster.

"Idiots."

She'd had a change of heart after she departed from Grey Cloak the last time. Tatiana infuriated her so much that she couldn't see straight. Anya had no faith at all in the Wizard Watch brood. She blamed them for the deaths of the Sky Riders as much as any. The Wizard Watch should have known. They should have warned them, but they didn't. It gnawed at her stomach.

At the same time, she didn't have a single friend she could count on aside from Cinder. She'd never been separated from him so long or so far either. He was her rock, and he was as far south as a dragon could be. He was at the Shelf, protecting his and Firestok's fledglings. Firestok, his wife, and her uncle Justus's dragon, had died at Gunder Island, killed by Black Frost himself.

I have to talk some sense into Grey Cloak. He must listen.

As the water carried her swiftly toward the bank, something tugged at her foot, like a fish nipping at a line. *What was that? A little late for fish to be biting.*

Whatever it was came back and swallowed her entire foot and tried to pull her down. She fastened herself to the log and held on for dear life. "Gah!"

Anya fought to hang on to the log as the thing below the surface weighed her down like an anchor. Her grip held fast as both she and the log were hauled down below the surface. She kicked with her free foot, but whatever the thing was would not give.

Up and down she bobbed in the surging water, unable to breathe. Her arms began to tire, and she was hauled down into the blackness of the river. She couldn't see a thing. The only thing that existed was whatever was pulling her down to a watery death. She hit the bottom, and a growing pressure crunched the plating around her calf. *Thunderbolts!*

Anya's well-honed training kicked in. She snatched her dagger free of her belt and filled the blade with a charge of energy. With her lungs starting to burn, she caught her first glimpse of the river monster. It looked like a catfish, as big as a cow and with spiny ridges all over, and tugged her to the muddy bottom.

She struck the burning dagger blade into the giant fish's skull. The first blow sank deep, but the foul creature held fast. She struck it again and again, but its firm jaws held.

Her chest burned, and she wanted to scream. Instead, she caught a glimpse of the wriggling water beast's gills and knew exactly what to do. She lashed out, the dagger exploded in the river monster's side, and its jaws popped open.

Anya kicked and swam away, only to have her armor drag her toward the bottom. With absolutely no sense of direction, she crawled along the bed of the river, praying that she was headed to safety.

Her lungs seemed to catch fire, and she couldn't take another breath. She desperately gasped for air. The black water swallowed her up, and her last breath escaped. Her life flashed before her eyes, her last thoughts of Cinder and Grey Cloak. The water abyss took her in, and she blacked out.

ANYA SAT UP, gasping for air. She was by a warm campfire, covered in dried river grit and trembling like a leaf. She panted. It was pitch black on a cloud-filled night, but at least it wasn't raining. She'd had enough water to last her the rest of her life.

She scanned the surrounding woodland and didn't see a soul. *What happened? Who saved me?* Someone had to have built that fire, but it wasn't her. *Who else could it have been? Did the river elves save me?*

Her sword belt lay by the fire, and she rolled over and grabbed it. She started to stand, but a fierce pain lanced through her leg, and she plopped down on her backside, wincing. A bandage covered the nasty river fish bite. She started to peel the bandage away.

"I wouldn't do that," someone said calmly.

She pulled her sword free of the sheath, glaring around, and said, "Show yourself."

"Why? So you can stab me?" The man speaking

stepped away from the shadow of the woodlands and into full view, illuminated by the fire.

He stood tall and rangy. His long hair was rusty brown with streaks of silvery white, and his brown eyes twinkled with gold in the firelight.

"Who are you?" Anya asked, her heart racing.

"I'm a friend." He knelt in front of her and offered his hand and a smile. "Call me Than."

Anya cast a wary eye at him. He had handsome features in his wrinkled face. His brown eyes were as warm as melted gold.

She took his hand. "Than, huh?"

"At your service," he said in a voice that carried strength and kindness. He hauled her up to her feet as easily as a man lifting a child. "A brave thing, trying to swim in your armor. I don't think it is meant to float."

"That wasn't my plan," she said, and more water drained out of her suit. Her first few steps made a squishy sound.

Than chuckled.

Anya removed one boot, poured the water out, and drained the other in the same fashion. Hopping on one foot, she shoved them both back on. "I appreciate the assistance, but I have to go."

"Yes, you have to catch up with your friends, Grey Cloak and Dyphestive. Lucky for you, I'm heading in the same direction."

Her brow furrowed, and her hand fell to the pommel of her dagger. It clicked out of the scabbard. "You have some explaining to do, friend."

Than nodded. "That I do. I'll explain along the journey. In the meantime, we must chase them quickly."

"Why is that?"

"Because wherever they go, trouble follows."

"You can say that again."

With surprising agility, the brawny man took off east.

The move caught Anya off guard. She sprinted after him, thinking, *Thunderbolts, he's fast!*

44

"Tatiana, I'm not going to be able to drive this wagon through that land," Crane said with a poke of his stubby index finger. "What madness overtook you that you would think I could make that passage?"

The Wild was a mass of huge trees and dense brush that barred any passage into the forest. Large insects hummed, and the chirps of loud birds came from within the leagues of leafy branches. The horses nickered and stamped their hooves.

Grey Cloak stood on the forest edge. He broke off a thorn of a rosebush as thick as his finger. It had a dewy drop on the end that he started to touch.

"Don't do that. It's a mild poison, not nectar, that will sting for days," Tatiana said.

"Thanks for the warning." He flicked the thorn away.

The treetops of the forest blotted out the morning sun, casting a leagues-long shadow over them. Whatever creatures were inside the womb of the forest didn't sound good either. The hard buzzing sounded like something drilling in his earhole. It reminded him of the jungle-forest outside of Hidemark but far more unpleasant. He thought of Anya and wished he'd taken her advice.

Crane sat on the wagon bench, rubbing his face. "There has to be another way around."

"You aren't obligated to go," Tatiana said with a stern look on her face. She covered it with a cotton cowl. "You can wait or go around and meet us on the north side of the Wild. You shouldn't have anything to fear from the East River elves. They are well aware of your presence now."

Crane's eyes popped. "Alone? You want me to travel alone. I must say, I've traveled plenty by myself but not in such wild lands. Not alone, ever. I'd prefer that someone went with me." He looked at the forest. "Certainly all of us don't need to go in there."

"I'll stay with you," Jakoby said. He unbuckled his sword belt and tossed it into the back of the wagon. "I admit I'm not fond of bugs of any sort."

"Stay north along the river. We will catch up with you at Staatus. It is a grand city. You will enjoy it," Tatiana offered.

Several horses whinnied, including the nightmare, Vixen.

Razor tugged at the reins of his horse and said, "I don't

think we are the only ones with an aversion to the forest. The beasts would rather take a pass as well."

"It's probably better that we travel on foot. It is possible that there will be climbing to do," Tatiana added. She caught everyone's distraught looks. "I'm sorry. This Wizard Watch is heavily guarded by the terrain. That is why few venture these paths."

"Then how do they get there?" Grey Cloak asked.

"This way or another," she said.

"Yes, the other way that you cannot say. Thank you so very much, Tatiana." He dismounted, giving her a disgusted look, and led the horse over to the wagon and tethered it to the back.

"What about you, Leena?" the deep-voiced Jakoby said. "Are you coming along with me or staying with them?"

Seated on her horse, Leena stared down Dyphestive and pointed him toward the wagon.

"Uh, I'm not going with Crane. I'm going with Grey Cloak."

Leena adamantly shook her head. She pointed at the wagon again.

Dyphestive stiffened. "No. I'm not going with Crane."

She pulled out her nunchaku.

"Uh-oh," Grey Cloak said as he backed away toward Zora. "Lovers' quarrel."

"It is not!" Dyphestive whined. "We aren't—well, I'm not even saying that."

Zora giggled as she dismounted. "This will prove interesting."

"Listen, Leena, you can whack me with your little sticks all you want, but it won't change my mind," Dyphestive said as he looked at Crane and Jakoby. "Either you're going with them, or you're coming with me."

Leena tucked her nunchaku back in her belt. She eyed Dyphestive, smiled, and bowed.

As Leena dismounted, Dyphestive mouthed, "Did I win?" to Grey Cloak.

Grey Cloak shrugged.

Jakoby said, "It's settled, then. Crane and I will take the horses to Staatus while the rest of you have all of the fun. Journey well."

"Aye, journey well," Crane said. With a flick of his carriage whip, they were off and rolling north, leaving the others in the grim shadows of the Wild.

Grey Cloak approached Tatiana and said, "Now that you've scared two of the company and the horses off, please take it upon yourself and lead the way."

Tatiana nodded at him and said, "Grunt. Make a path."

Without hesitation, Grunt plowed twenty feet into the thorn-rich shrubs, clearing a path for all of them to walk through. The company had made it into the vine-rich terrain when the steady buzzing quieted. An eerie silence fell across the forest, and it was so quiet that one could hear a leaf drop.

Grey Cloak looked at Tatiana and said, "Well done. *It knows we are here.*"

"Are you scared, Grey Cloak?" Tatiana asked.

"No." He glanced upward. Small creatures were jumping from branch to branch. They were like monkeys or squirrels, but they could have been anything. He stood touching shoulders with Zora, feeling like he'd crossed into another world. The trees dwarfed them like ants, and a caterpillar as long as his arms snaked between red ferns taller than a man.

A crunching sound came from down at his feet. Streak was eating a beetle with a horned nose and speckled bright-yellow wings. The loud sound drew everyone's stare.

"Well, that's one less bug for us to worry about," he said in a nervous but cheery voice. "It doesn't look like much daylight is going to shine on our path. Tatiana, why don't you shine some light on our dreary setting."

Tatiana lifted the Star of Light over her head. A soft white light illuminated the dimness, exposing the colorful flora that surrounded them. "Better?" she asked.

"Better." He nodded.

A distant bestial roar echoed through the woodland, scattering the keet birds nestled in the branches.

Grey Cloak eyed Tatiana and asked, "Is that your mother calling?"

45

"Hold still," Grey Cloak said to Zora. A green-eyed fly bigger than a bullfrog was on her back.

Zora froze. "What is it?"

"It's nothing. I'll take care of it." Oversize flies and mosquitos were all over the treacherous forest, causing the alarming buzz that harassed their senses. Quicker than a cat, he batted the fly down and squished it under his boot. "Uck."

Zora sneered as she watched him wipe the bug guts off his boots on a patch of moss. "That is nasty. This place is nasty." Her face was beaded with sweat, and locks of her damp hair clung to her forehead. "The Wizard Watch had better have a place to bathe."

Tatiana passed by both of them. She'd wrapped herself

up in her cloak like a blanket and covered most of her face with a cowl. "It will."

"Look at me. My clothes are soaked through with stinking sweat." Zora swatted at some sort of purple beetle that hovered near her face. "Ew... what is that?" She back-handed it away.

"I don't know. I've never seen bugs like this before. Or so big either." He hooked her arm. "Come on, I'll protect you."

Talon had been walking for hours in the sweltering willowwhacks. Along the way, they'd killed more than their fair share of nasty bugs. The only one of them that appeared to enjoy it was Streak, who feasted on almost everything they killed.

Grunt led the way, powering through thick brush where needed. Like Streak, he appeared unfazed. As for the rest of them, they were drenched in their own sweat as they lumbered along with long faces.

Razor walked behind Grunt, Dyphestive and Leena behind them, with Tatiana in the middle and Grey Cloak and Zora bringing up the rear. As bad as the trek was, daylight sometimes spilled through the leaves, and they would take a moment to bask in it before moving on. Otherwise, the Wild remained damp and gloomy, dripping with misery.

"Tatiana, I have to ask." Grey Cloak fanned a mosquito

away from his eyes. "How is it that you know exactly where you are going if you've never been this way before?"

"I know. We all know. To our kind, the Wizard Watch is a beacon. I can feel where it is in my bones. A guiding light," Tatiana said.

"I see. It's very strange that the other Wizard Watch I've seen was not hidden. It was in plain sight." He was speaking of his encounter at one of the wizard towers when he first adventured with Talon and they met at a Wizard Watch in Sulter Slay. "Why is this one hidden? Are they all hidden?"

"No." Tatiana pushed tall ferns up and aside so Grey Cloak and Zora could pass. "And this one is not hidden. It was built where it stands, and the Wild grew around it over the centuries. I can't explain it. None can. It is this way."

"Oh, well, that is very helpful. Thank you for that wonderful explanation."

"I cannot control the terrain. I can only control my mouth," Tatiana said.

"Har-har."

Tatiana hooked his arm and brought him to a stop. "I don't know which is worse, the buzzing bugs or your complaintive lips. Grey Cloak, no one made you come this way. It was your choice. I'm guiding you. If you want to turn back now, you can. But I am going forward."

Everyone in the company had stopped and looked at him. They had tired eyes, stooped shoulders, and a growing sense of irritation on their faces. Even the bugs stopped buzzing.

Grey Cloak shooed her with his hands and said, "Lead the way, Tat."

She nodded and went on her way.

Zora nudged him. "It's time you laid off."

"I know, but I can't help myself around her. She irritates me."

"Be the bigger elf," Zora offered, "because all of your complaining isn't very attractive."

He raised an eyebrow. *I'd better remember that.*

They journeyed another hour or so until they came upon a steep climb. Using the vines that snaked over the slippery ground, they hauled themselves to the top.

Trailing far behind the others, Grey Cloak caught the sound of cascading water and exchanged excited glances with Zora. At the top of the hill, brilliant light shone through a break in the trees. He redoubled his efforts, and with a spring in his step, he hurried up while saying to Zora, "See you at the top."

"Not if I see you first." Zora took off right after.

Grey Cloak beat her up the hillside by five strides and met up with the others at the top of the ridge. Every person stood quietly, staring with wonder at a gorgeous watery oasis.

Dyphestive was the first one to strip down to his

trousers and jump into the crystal-blue pond. "Waaah-hoo!"

"No, wait!" Tatiana warned.

It was too late. Dyphestive splashed into the water, soaking everyone standing on the rim, but mostly Tatiana.

46

Everyone stripped out of their heavy gear and waded into the serenity of the bubbling pond. Tiny bubbles fizzed to the top when they entered, and red-and-green-speckled frogs jumped from lily pad to lily pad.

Beautiful willow trees grew inside the breathtaking pond, their roots and branches making comfortable nooks to lie upon. Tatiana, Zora, and Leena waded underneath the leafy trees, washing their sweat off with the clean water. Razor and Grunt splashed one another until Grunt practically drowned Razor by creating a huge wave with his arms.

Dyphestive spit a stream of water out of his mouth into Grey Cloak's face. Grey Cloak wiped it away and brushed his damp locks behind his ears. Streak swam toward him, flat head just above the water, tail swishing behind him like a gator. He plucked his dragon out of the water and tossed him back in, splashing the women.

"Stop it!" Zora said, as she rubbed her eyes with her fists. "You got water in my mouth. And it doesn't taste as good as it looks." Her nose crinkled. "It's thick."

He splashed another wave at her. "What difference does it make? You're all wet anyway."

"Will you let me relax?"

He shrugged. "Certainly." As soon as she vanished beneath the leafy willow trees, he ducked under the water and swam after her. He snuck right behind her, popped up, grabbed her, and dunked her.

Zora popped out of the water, gasping, hair covering her eyes, and said, "I'm going to kill you!" She jumped on his back and hauled him down into the pond.

They were both laughing when he slung his hair back and said, "All right, we're even." He offered his hand. "Shake."

"In your dreams," Zora said. She gently splashed him. "Go away."

In the meantime, Dyphestive crept behind Leena. She watched out of the corners of her eyes. The moment he grabbed her, she flipped his manly frame into the water. He rose with her on his back, locking him in a choke hold.

Dyphestive clawed at the air and said in a raspy voice, "It's only a game. Leena, let go."

Leena bit his ear.

"Ow! Did she bite my ear?"

"I think it was a love bite," Grey Cloak said as he shifted, trying to get a better look at Leena. "She might be smiling too. Hard to tell with her wooden expression, but I believe she is having fun with you."

"I hope so." Dyphestive carried Leena on his broad back like a child and waded deeper into the water.

Zora backed into Grey Cloak's arms and had him wrap his arms around her. "This is nice, isn't it?"

Grey Cloak had a catch in his throat as a result of her move catching him off guard and awkwardly said, "Yes?"

She turned her head. "What's wrong? You swallow too much pond water?"

He cleared his throat and gave her a squeeze. "Maybe, or you took my breath away."

"Ha-ha, but I liked it." She sank deeper into his arms.

Grey Cloak wasn't sure what was happening. He was warm all over, and his cheeks were as warm as toast. *This is wonderful.*

Tatiana wandered by without giving them a glance. She moved with the grace and beauty of a swan, and her wet clothing clung to every curve of her figure.

Grey Cloak found it difficult to peel his eyes away from her, though the prickly elf so easily got under his skin. He shook his head and blinked. *I feel so good.*

"Look at the birds," Zora said dreamily as she watched the waterfowl fly from branch to branch. "So amazing."

The sun bleeding through the branches started to fade. Tatiana, who was standing in the middle of the pond, let out a bloodcurdling scream. Grey Cloak thrust his body from underneath the willow trees, tugging Zora along.

Tatiana's mouth gaped as she stood still, looking down on the grime that covered her body. The clear pond water appeared to be nothing more than swamp sludge with slimy beds of algae floating on the top. She trembled as she slung it off of her.

"What's happening?" Grey Cloak asked as he scanned the once-sumptuous cove. Where the sunlight shone, the pond appeared to be a sanctuary of refreshing conditions, but where the shadows hit, a darker appearance was revealed.

The pond turned ugly and muddy. The willow trees' leaves hanging down in the water were withering and dying, choked out by thick vines coiled around the trunk and winding into the branches. Steam began to rise from the water, and a putrid smell caused everyone to cover their noses as they backed into the spots of light.

Everyone desperately started wiping the grime from their bodies. The bright spots of sun were quickly diminishing.

"Grey Cloak, what is this?" Zora asked in a shaky voice as she flicked an ugly toad from her shoulder. "Ew!"

An eight-foot-long ringed snake casually cut through the murk and swam right between them.

Zora hid behind Grey Cloak, shoulders shaking like a leaf. "I hate snakes. We need to get out of here."

"I'm with you." He took her hand and pulled her toward the bank. "Let's go."

"Everyone!" Tatiana called. "Get out of the pond. Move!"

The sunlight was blotted out by treetops that merged on their own, and the beautiful pond was covered in darkness so black that everyone stopped.

Grey Cloak felt Zora's heart beating, and her fingernails dug into his hand. "Everyone, remain still," he said, searching through the darkness.

All of a sudden, several dull lights shone from the pond's bank, illuminating three rawboned men with sunken eyes and oversize pointed ears protruding through their long strands of stringy white-gray hair that hung to their toes. Their flowing beards were long, covering their chests and touching the backs of the great bearded elk they sat upon. They scanned the pond with haunted expressions and carried gnarled wooden staffs in their bony hands. A sour yellow light was nestled in the top of the staffs, casting an eerie light on the company.

Tatiana backed away from the bank and said, "Don't let them touch you. They are the Wizzlum."

"What is a Wizzlum?" Grey Cloak asked.

Tatiana swallowed and said, "Life-draining druids."

47

The last window of sunlight was closed off by the trees, leaving the company standing flat-footed in the murky, smelly grime.

Grey Cloak's neck hairs stood on end as the Wizzlum lifted the glowing heads of their staffs. "Run!" he called.

His boots stuck in the pond's scummy bottom. He wasn't alone, either, as the others fought and splashed against the icky pond's grip.

"Something has me!" Tatiana cried. Her body was jerked neck deep into the water. Her hand thrashed above the surface. She bobbed violently up and down, gulping in the foul water.

The pond came alive from all directions. Algae clung to their bodies like sweat. The vines in the willow branches dropped, snaked through the water, and seized the company's arms and legs.

A vine coiled around Grey Cloak's wrist. He jerked and pulled his hand free, but another vine immediately entwined itself around his other wrist. "Madness!" He snatched a dagger from its sheath and sawed at the vine. The sharp blade cut but slowly.

Snap! Snap! Snap! Nearby, wading waist deep in the water, Dyphestive and Grunt yanked the vines out of the trees.

Dyphestive plowed through the foaming water. "Tatiana, hang on!"

Her head sank into the blackness of the pond, leaving bubbles behind.

"Get her, Dyphestive!" Grey Cloak called. "Hang on, Tat!"

More vines than he could count sprang out of the water and struck at him like snakes. He grabbed Zora, whose fingers clutched for him. "I have you!"

The vines slithered around their bodies and began to constrict.

Zora gasped. "Guh!"

Every member of Talon was neck deep in the murk. Even the massive Grunt thrashed wildly.

Razor struck out with his blades, chopping off bits of the vine's slimy fibers. "What sort of enemy is this? I fight enemies with swords, not weeds!" The bright steel of his sword flashed repeatedly, until the vines snagged his arms and squeezed. "Filthy weeds!"

The haunting faces of the Wizzlum did not change, and they and their elks did not move an inch. They were the last things Grey Cloak saw before the great vines pulled him under.

Nooo! Grey Cloak's fingers fought for the inner pockets of his cloak. *I need the figurine!*

The unnatural strength of the vines pulled his arms back.

He summoned the wizardry. His fingers caught fire, and he latched them around one of the vines, sending a charge of fire blasting through its fibers. The water boiled, and the vine caught fire. The flames spread up the length of the vine and spread to the branches.

Grey Cloak and Zora burst out of the pond, gasping.

An awful sound followed. "*Skreeeyeeelll!*" The vines twisted, reared, and splashed in the water. They flicked out, attacking like snakes again.

Grey Cloak's hand felt like it was on fire. If not for the water, it would have been burned to a crisp. He desperately unleashed a charge into the vines and glared at the Wizzlum. "Don't mess with me. Let us go."

The stoic druids sat on their beasts, as composed as ever, but the one in the middle said, "This is our swamp, not yours. We do as we please. Tonight, we feast on intruders."

"Not if I have anything to say about it!" Grey Cloak answered.

"Grey Cloak, look out!" Zora said.

He turned around just in time to see a bunch of vines coming at him, and they swallowed his body entirely.

48

Talon was tethered to the bearded elk and dragged through the forest, leaves sticking to their grimy bodies. Each of them was bound with thick vines. They were hauled into a dark cave lit by smokeless torches on the walls and abandoned.

After the Wizzlum departed, Grey Cloak pushed himself into a sitting position. "Is everyone well?"

"I am," Dyphestive said. His neck muscles bulged as he strained to break free of the vines. "Guh! These vines are thick! I can't budge them."

"You don't have any leverage," Razor said. He rolled over the ground until he hit the rough cave wall. "Cripes, I can't get out of this cocoon." He eyed Grey Cloak. "How'd you do it?"

"I don't know," Grey Cloak replied as he eyeballed his

surroundings.

Everyone was lying on the ground as if they'd been rolled up in blankets. They could only wiggle their fingers and toes. Tatiana and Leena lay facing each other. They looked like they'd been cast aside. Grunt was face-first in the dirt, hooves roughly kicking as he fought to roll over to his back. Zora lay quietly beside Grey Cloak, staring up at the roots that were growing out of the high ceiling.

"Where do you think your cousins went, Tatiana?" Grey Cloak asked.

"They aren't my cousins," Tatiana replied. "I wish you would quit saying things like that. This isn't my fault."

He rolled his eyes. "Of course not."

"What is that supposed to mean?"

"Don't even start bickering, you two," Zora warned. "We need to find a way out of here. Use your energy on that."

"Agreed," Tatiana said.

Leena was giving her a hard-eyed stare.

"Will you close your eyes or at least blink? You're giving me shivers, Leena."

Leena didn't move.

"Grey, how are we going to get out of here?" Dyphestive asked. He writhed and flexed in his bonds. "I can't break them, and Grunt can't either. The vines flex and constrict, like living things."

"I'll think of something," he said. He didn't have any ideas at the moment. Using wizardry might burn the vines, but without water, it might burn his hands too. Shifting his shoulders, he tried to wriggle free. The vines tightened. *Ow!* "Tatiana, what are these druids? Can't we reason with them? After all, they are elves, aren't they?"

"They are the Wizzlum. Don't call them elves unless you want to make it worse," Tatiana said as he managed to roll away from Leena's glare. "They might be elven of a sort but claim to be their own race. We came upon them at the most unfortunate time." She spit a piece of a wet leaf out of her mouth. "They are feeding."

Dread overcame Grey Cloak. "Feeding? This forest is filled with animals. Why would they feed on us?"

"Because they love the wildlife more than men. They consider all of the races evil."

"They are a race too. Who are they to judge?" Dyphestive asked.

Tatiana shrugged. "They do what they do. Regardless, if we don't find a way out of here soon, they will drain us like a spider sucking out bug juice."

Zora cringed. "Ew."

Razor rolled over until he got a good look at Tatiana and said, "Well, isn't that great. Can't you use your magic star to get us out of here?"

"I could if I could reach it," she said. "But as you can see, my hands are fastened the same as yours."

"Coming your way." Razor started rolling toward

Tatiana. Determined, he didn't stop until he bumped into her. His fingers wiggled at his sides. "How about this?"

Her eyes widened. "That's not where it is."

"Are you sure?" Razor replied.

"I'm sure. Lower, much lower, at my waist."

Quickly grasping the futility of Razor's attempt, Grey Cloak hopped from flat on his back to his feet. With his thighs bound down to the knees, he baby-stepped toward the exit.

Tree roots and twisting black vines blocked the exit. Grey Cloak bumped up against them, but they were as hard as steel. "Isn't that peculiar," he said.

"Can't you get out?" Zora asked.

He shook his head. "Not without an ax or fire."

"Gah! I can't get it, Tatiana," Razor grumbled. "Those vines squeeze whenever I touch them. "Cursed things. When we get out of here, I'm going to burn them. Burn them all."

The roots blocking the cave's exit parted.

Grey Cloak stood face to face with three Wizzlum. "We were wondering when dinner might be served."

With a gentle motion of his staff, one of the Wizzlum flung Grey Cloak across the room, making him slam into the wall. He bounced off and rolled beside Zora.

"Dinner," Zora said to him. "Really? And you hardly eat."

With a groan, he twisted around until he saw them again. "It seemed like a good thing to say at the time."

The three creepy, long-bearded druids entered the room. Their raggedy earthen robes dragged over the ground as they approached. As their haunting eyes swept over their prisoners, the long-eared leader in the front poked his bony finger at Grunt.

"What are they doing?" Zora whispered.

"I don't know."

The two Wizzlum in the rear waved the glowing tips of their sticks at Grunt. His big body was towed across the floor by an unseen force that sent chills down Grey Cloak's spine. Grunt lay in front of the druids with his head rolling from side to side, his huge brown eyes staring up at them.

Two druids poked their staffs into Grunt's body and pinned him to the ground. The leader knelt behind Grunt's head and lay his staff on his chest. The putrid yellow gems cradled in the staffs glowed brighter. The lead Wizzlum fastened his crooked fingers to Grunt's head, and Grunt lurched.

Razor said warily, "What are they doing to him?"

Grunt started to convulse.

Tatiana looked on in horror and said, "They are draining his essence."

49

With his fingers locked on Grunt's skull, the Wizzlum leader's eyes started to glow hot white. Grunt's back arched, and he let out quick, painful grunts. His big body twitched and spasmed. The other pair of Wizzlum druids drove the glowing tips of their staffs into him, pinning him fast to the ground.

"What are you *doing* to him?" Razor screamed. "Quit that! I'll kill you for it!"

Hot, pungent air blasted through the chamber the moment the leader of the three Wizzlum opened his mouth. They all muttered as one in a threatening, tense, and garbled tone.

"Do something, Tatiana," Grey Cloak pleaded.

"I can't," she responded. "I'm sorry."

Grunt's body was lifted off the floor by an invisible

force. The hairs on his arms stood on end, and his tense muscles began to shrink under his shriveling skin.

"No!" Razor hollered. "Nooo!"

All of a sudden, the Wizzlums' wispy hair started to thicken and turn brown. Their pale skin ripened, and sinew began to build underneath. Their heads cocked back, and their hungry eyes radiated with triumph.

Grey Cloak's skin crawled as he watched Grunt's mighty body begin to shrivel. *I have to do something.* He didn't have the Figurine of Heroes in hand, but he knew the spell-casting words. He started to say them.

From out of nowhere, a small vine coiled around his mouth and silenced the mystic words. *Nooo!*

He caught Zora's wide eyes. He'd never seen such fear before or felt such spine-chilling terror. His heart raced. He couldn't believe the horror he was seeing.

A roar rumbled through the cave. The Wizzlums' deep moaning came to an abrupt stop.

Grunt's body crashed to the floor, sagging inside the vines, unmoving.

The Wizzlum stood. No longer were they hunched. Their limbs were strong and their features far younger and full. They set their piercing eyes on the entrance to the chamber.

Streak crept inside, his tongue flicking.

Grey Cloak bit into the vine over his mouth. He wanted nothing more than to save his dragon from an inevitable life-draining doom. *Get out of here, Streak! Get out of here!*

The leader of the Wizzlum bent a knee before Streak. With staff in hand, the silent killer beckoned the dragon over.

Streak wandered over to the druid, pink tongue flicking out of his mouth, as innocent as a hungry puppy. He stopped a few feet short of the druid.

"Get away from him, Streak! Get away!" Dyphestive called. No sooner had he spoken than finger-thick vines covered his mouth, silencing him.

Before the others could utter a word, twisting vines covered their mouths and silenced them too.

The Wizzlum leader stretched out his long arm and beckoned Streak closer. Grey Cloak swallowed. Tatiana had assured him that the Wizzlum valued creatures over people, but he had no idea whether that included dragons or not. *Run, Streak, run!*

Streak glanced in Grey Cloak's direction, and one of the dragon's eyelids flicked like a wink.

Huh? Is he trying to tell me something?

As if on command, Streak lowered his flat head to the ground in a bowing motion. The leader leaned closer.

Streak, no bigger than a small hound, opened his wide jaws, and his belly filled with air. The leader of the Wizzlum leaned back, and the tip of his staff brightened.

Blue flames spewed out of Streak's mouth and engulfed

the Wizzlum's tattered robes and long hair. Streak poured it on, turning the man into burning flesh.

The heat on Grey Cloak's face sent new life coursing through his extremities. The entangling vines loosed their hold, and he started to wriggle free.

One of the Wizzlum crept up behind Streak with his glowing staff poised to strike.

Grey Cloak tried to shout, "Watch out!" But he was too late.

A flashing sword cleaved the Wizzlum's head from his shoulders. Standing behind the falling druid was Anya, a glimmering dragon sword in her hand.

The last druid charged her.

Anya ran her blade straight into his chest. She shoved the dead druid off with her boot and said, "Creepy."

The vines that bound the company began to loosen and fall away.

Grey Cloak flagged Streak over and asked, "Anya, where did you come from?"

"Outside," she said as she wiped her blade off on the dead druid's back.

He cradled Streak. "Another surprise from you, little dragon, but this time, I'm not as surprised as the last."

"Grunt! Grunt!" Razor rushed over and fell on the withered body of the minotaur. "Breathe, Grunt! Breathe!"

Than entered the chamber and caught everyone's eye. He said, "I took care of the rest." He tossed his long hair over his shoulder, knelt by Grunt, and placed his scaly hands on his chest.

"Can you save him?" Razor asked, his voice cracking.

Than gave Razor a sad look and said, "I wish I could, but he's too far gone. I'll help you bury him."

50

"That's one big grave," Grey Cloak commented quietly to Zora.

She nodded.

Outside of the Wizzlum caves, in a grove of yellow branch elms, Dyphestive was neck deep in the wide grave, shoveling out mounds of dirt with a somber expression. He'd been digging nonstop for over an hour, taking turns with Than and Razor but still carrying the bulk of the load. His hair was dirty, and he had dried grime from the sludge pond coating him all over.

All of them were filthy, except for Anya and Than, who stood with their toes on the grave's rim. They'd said little since they arrived.

Razor sniffled. He was sitting beside Grunt's shrunken body, wiping his eyes from time to time.

Tatiana hovered behind him with a hand on his shoulder. "I'm sorry," she said once again. "He was a true friend and protector."

"Yeah, I'll miss him." Razor wiped his eyes and stood. Eyeing the grave, he said, "I think that hole is big enough."

Dyphestive nodded, tossed the shovel aside, and climbed out.

Grey Cloak, Dyphestive, Than, and Razor each grabbed one of Grunt's limbs and carried him to the grave. He was as heavy as damp wood, and after a nod from Razor, they dropped him. *Thud.*

An uncomfortable silence followed. Everyone stood around the grave, looking down at Grunt.

Grey Cloak's throat tightened. Guilt built in his gut. Another companion had died on account of their excursions. "Would anyone like to say a few words?"

Razor put his hand over his heart. His eyes watered, and he wiped the tears with his thumb.

Dyphestive cleared his throat and said, "His life was too short lived."

"How old was he?" Zora asked politely.

Razor managed a shrug as his chest and shoulders trembled.

"I don't know," Tatiana said. Her breath hitched as she sighed. "But I was under the impression he was young."

"I hope he's in a better place now," Razor muttered. "May he freely roam the greenest pastures for all eternity."

"Well said," Than added. He bent over, plucked the shovel from the ground, and started digging into the mounds of dirt.

Razor stopped him and said, "Let me do it."

THE FIRST TIME Grey Cloak had laid eyes on a Wizard Watch tower was back in Sulter Slay when he'd first joined up with Talon. It was a great stone tower with unique architecture, standing several stories high. It was in a valley in a field of dragon bones. Its stone walls were blackened by fire, and no entrance showed.

The tower east of Great River was little different. It was another marvel of stone architecture that reached toward the clouds. It was made from large granite blocks and circled by rings of smooth columns. Beams of sunlight leaked through the passing clouds, showing off the stone in the purest elemental white.

In the fields surrounding the tower were deposits of colorful rocks that glowed with vibrant life of their own. They were pink, yellow, bright blue, and emerald green and were roughhewn, jagged but as beautiful as gemstones.

Talon stood on a rise, looking up at the wizardly wonder. Despite the otherworldly design, it was a cold, unwelcoming building with no doorway insight. Additionally, it was surrounded by a ring of thorn bushes taller than men and many yards deep. Black crows and tiny birds flew in and out of it.

Grey Cloak broke a thorn off a bush and eyed it. A dew drop dripped from the thorn's tip. "It looks like you are home, Tatiana."

"Wait here," she replied. She stood in front of the barrier of thorns. Several moments later, the thorns parted and opened up a path. "I'll return... soon."

Tatiana headed down the path, and as she did so, the thorn barrier closed behind her. She emerged on the other side of the path, walking up the hill toward the tower. Her shapely figure diminished the closer she came to the ominous tower, and she vanished before she touched its sleek walls.

Grey Cloak rubbed his forehead and said, "I don't know about you, but my skull isn't aching anymore."

Zora nudged his ribs with her knuckles. "Let it rest. She's gone."

Seeing Zora's exhausted expression, he nodded.

The company made a campfire on the edge of the woodland. All eyes were on the tower as the sun started to set again.

"An eerie place to be," Razor murmured as he poked a stick in the fire.

Dyphestive's belly grumbled so loudly that Leena stood. She shook her head and patted her belly.

"Yes, I'm hungry. I hope Tatiana brings us back something to eat."

Leena pointed at the woodland.

Dyphestive shook his head. "I'm not hunting."

Leena pointed again.

He shook his head again. "Not now."

"It looks like someone is squabbling with their lover," Grey Cloak said.

"Don't say that." Dyphestive looked embarrassed. "She's not my—" He caught Leena's eyes and said, "Never mind." He rose. "I'll try to find something to eat."

"Look," Razor said.

Everyone turned toward the barrier of thorns. It split open again, and Tatiana approached. She was clean from head to toe, without a smudge of sludge on her.

As Zora stood, she crossed her arms and said, "Well, don't you look refreshed."

"The Wizard Watch requires standards when one communes with them," Tatiana said politely.

Grey Cloak stepped forward and said, "That's wonderful for you, but what about the rest of us?"

"I need you and Dyphestive to come with me. The rest of you will have to wait," Tatiana said.

"How long?" Grey Cloak asked.

"The Wizard Watch did not say. They only requested to see you and Dyphestive." Tatiana's demeanor was more wooden than frigid.

Dyphestive stood by his brother's side and said, "If we go, we all go."

Tatiana shook her head. "That cannot be at the moment. I'm sorry. You have to trust me."

"Grunt dies on this trek, and this is the treatment we get? Everyone is left stranded among the thorns?"

Anya walked out of the woodland's edge and said, "This is exactly what you should expect. You don't need to go in there, either of you. You can't trust them."

"You can trust me," Tatiana assured them.

Grey Cloak knelt, gathered Streak in his arms, and stood. "Can I take him?"

Tatiana nodded.

He looked up at Dyphestive. "What do you say?"

"I go where you go," Dyphestive replied.

"Fine. Tatiana, lead the way."

Anya hooked his arm. "Remember who you are." She eyed Dyphestive. "Both of you. And don't forget."

"Forget what?" Grey Cloak asked.

She looked him dead in the eye and said, "I warned you."

CAN Grey Cloak and Dyphestive trust Tatiana?

What horror's lie inside of the Wizard watch?

Will the outcome change everyone's lives forever?

Don't miss the next riveting book! Details below!

PLEASE LEAVE A REVIEW FOR BATTLEGROUND. THEY ARE A HUGE HELP! LINK!

WIZARD WATCH: Dragon Wars #8, on sale now!

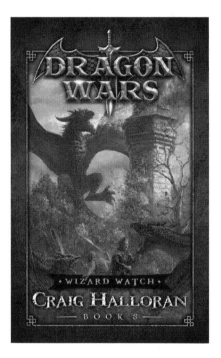

AND IF YOU haven't already, signup for my newsletter and grab 3 FREE books including the Dragon Wars Prequel.
WWW.DRAGONWARSBOOKS.COM

TEACHERS AND STUDENTS, if you would like to order paperback copies for you library or classroom, email craig@thedarkslayer.com to receive a special discount.

GEAR UP in this Dragon Wars body armor enchanted with a +2 Coolness factor/+4 at Gaming Conventions. Sizes range from halfling (Small) to Ogre (XXL). LINK .
www.society6.com

ABOUT THE AUTHOR

*On Facebook, you can find me at The Darkslayer Report or Craig Halloran.*Check me out on BookBub and follow: HalloranOnBookBub.

*I'd love it if you would subscribe to my mailing list: www.craighalloran.com.

*Twitter, Twitter, Twitter. I am there, too: www. twitter.com/CraigHalloran.

*And of course, you can always email me at craig@thedarkslayer.com.

See my book lists below!

ALSO BY CRAIG HALLORAN

book series)

The Odyssey of Nath Dragon Series (New Series) (Prequel to Chronicles of Dragon)

The Darkslayer Series 1 (6-book series)

Wrath of the Royals (Book 1)

Blades in the Night (Book 2)

Underling Revenge (Book 3)

Danger and the Druid (Book 4)

Outrage in the Outlands (Book 5)

Chaos at the Castle (Book 6)

Boxset 1-3

Boxset 4-6

Omnibus 1-6

The Darkslayer: Bish and Bone, Series 2 (10-book series)

Bish and Bone (Book 1)

Black Blood (Book 2)

Red Death (Book 3)

Lethal Liaisons (Book 4)

Torment and Terror (Book 5)

Brigands and Badlands (Book 6)

War in the Wasteland (Book 7)

Slaughter in the Streets (Book 8)

Hunt of the Beast (Book 9)

The Battle for Bone (Book 10)

Boxset 1-5

Boxset 6-10

Bish and Bone Omnibus (Books 1-10)

CLASH OF HEROES: Nath Dragon Meets The Darkslayer mini series

Book 1

Book 2

Book 3

The Henchmen Chronicles

The King's Henchmen

The King's Assassin

The King's Prisoner

The King's Conjurer

The King's Enemies

The King's Spies

The Gamma Earth Cycle

Escape from the Dominion

Flight from the Dominion

Prison of the Dominion

The Supernatural Bounty Hunter Files (10-book series)

Smoke Rising: Book 1

I Smell Smoke: Book 2

Where There's Smoke: Book 3

Smoke on the Water: Book 4

Smoke and Mirrors: Book 5

Up in Smoke: Book 6

Smoke Signals: Book 7

Holy Smoke: Book 8

Smoke Happens: Book 9

Smoke Out: Book 10

Boxset 1-5

Boxset 6-10

Collector's Edition 1-10

Zombie Impact Series

Zombie Day Care: Book 1

Zombie Rehab: Book 2

Zombie Warfare: Book 3

Boxset: Books 1-3

OTHER WORKS & NOVELLAS

The Red Citadel and the Sorcerer's Power